SYDNEY SCOTT

EVERNIGHT PUBLISHING ®

www.evernightpublishing.com

SYDNEY SCOTT

DEDICATION

For my fellow cycle breakers. Doing the hard work is worth the effort.

SYDNEY SCOTT

WORTH THE EFFORT

Sun Valley, 3

Sydney Scott

Copyright © 2024

Chapter One
Caitlin

Eleven Years Ago

The envelope is clutched so tightly in my hands that it crumples slightly. Panicking, I smooth it out as I walk toward the school library, my home away from home. It's the last tutoring session I'll have with Noah Hunter, and I've finally decided to tell him how I feel. Well, I wrote how I feel in a letter and I'm going to give it to him today, which is about as brave as I can get. If I tried to speak my love for him, I'm not sure anything but stammering would come out, and this is too important to screw up. Noah leaves for college soon, and it's my last chance to express the feelings I've had for some time, the love I've felt for him over the last few months.

I started tutoring Noah in math at the beginning of

the school year as part of my volunteer hours for National Honor Society. I'm a junior, so I was able to get into the program even though I'm only sixteen years old. I skipped a grade in elementary and I'm the youngest junior in the school. Being the youngest and one of the smartest in my classes hasn't won me many friends. In fact, most kids my age think I'm too geeky, and the kids in my class think I'm too young. I'm kind of trapped between worlds and neither one wants me. I didn't have many companions growing up either, so I always spent my free time in the library where I could escape into all the different stories on the shelves. This led to a lifelong love of books and the library itself—it was my safe haven. It still is, but now it's also the place where I fell for Noah Hunter, the most amazing boy I've ever met.

Noah came in for tutoring about a month after the school year started. He wasn't doing so well in his pre-calculus class and needed to keep his grade up to stay on the football team. He was the star quarterback and helped our football team get to the playoffs last year. I never followed the sport much myself, but it's impossible not to know about it when football has such a massive student fan base, and Noah is one of the most popular boys in the school. He has a loyal following of other football players and cheerleaders that hang on his every word. I'm no different now, really. I could sit and listen to Noah talk about everything and nothing for hours, but I didn't belong to his crowd. I was the shy, geeky girl who was a little too smart and not very adept at socializing, so I loved him and cheered him on from the sidelines.

Our tutoring sessions started out normally enough, me showing him how to solve calculus problems and him trying his best to follow my instructions. He was a hard worker, and I admired that. No matter how frustrating he found a problem, he kept working at it until he got it right. One day in the fall, he remarked on the t-shirt I was wearing. It was a Batman t-shirt and he commented on how he loved superhero cartoons. We started talking about other things we had in common, which was surprisingly a lot. We both loved all things superhero, though we disagreed on which was better, Marvel or DC. He told me how he moved around a lot growing up and this school was the first he really felt a part of. I could certainly identify with that and told him how I never really felt a part of anything, even my own family. He listened intently and was always very kind to me. If we saw each other in the halls, I would wave and he would do that nod that cool guys do. Falling in love with Noah was easy, but now came the hard part—telling him.

The school is fairly empty this morning as class doesn't start for another hour or so. Wrenching open the heavy metal door to the library, I immediately find our usual table by the window where I sit and set up my notebooks and pencils. I slip the envelope containing my declaration under my folder. I'll give it to him toward the end of our session, that way he can read it and if things don't go well, I can just run off to class. My body feels anxious, my heart beating much too fast, and I fidget in my chair as I wait for Noah to arrive, my knees bouncing up and down and my foot tapping the worn carpet repeatedly. My fingers smooth over the legs of my jeans and pull at the hem of my plain white t-shirt before I adjust the frames of my black-rimmed glasses and run a hand over my unruly red curls. I tried to do my best with them this morning, but I'm sure they're as frizzy as they normally are. Noah won't care, though. I can tell he likes me for me, and I am very hopeful about how he'll feel when I give him my letter. The football season ended months ago and he could have stopped coming to tutoring, but I think he still does because he likes me as much as I like him. That's the hope, anyway.

The door to the library swings open and Noah saunters in. If my eyes hadn't already been glued to the door in anticipation of his arriving, they would have been drawn to him regardless. It's impossible not to stare at such a beautiful person. His jeans and black t-shirt mold perfectly to his athletic frame. His brown hair is a little longer than it was at the start of the year, just reaching down to his ears, and it looks a bit disheveled, but he tucks it back and smooths it out when he sees me. His smile widens as he makes his way over to our table and sits down across from me, placing his books and folders on the table with a wink in my direction. "What's up, Caity-bug? You ready to smarten me up a bit?" I love that he has a little nickname for me and it sounds so good with the lilt of his Texan accent. I can feel my cheeks heat, but I try to reel myself in and roll my eyes at him.

"You're already smart, Noah, and you know it. You just keep coming to tutoring because you like hanging out with me." Look at me, flirting like a normal person.

He sits back in his chair. "I do like hanging out with you. You're, like, the only person who actually listens when I talk," he says, a small smile playing across his beautiful, full lips.

I roll my eyes once more. "Please, you have people hanging over you all the time. You're not exactly hurting for attention." I certainly pay attention, and I know for a fact I'm not the only one.

"You jealous, Caity-bug?" His hazel eyes sparkle and he leans in a little closer. "You want to be the only one to give me attention?" His low voice is doing weird things to me. Goose bumps break out across my skin and my heart skips a beat. I know I am blushing fiercely and am in danger of blurting out my feelings, but instead of doing something disastrous like that, I pull out the math book we normally work from and try to change the subject.

Smiling, I clear my throat. "How about we both put our attention into this math book? It's our last session after all, so we better make it count." In more ways than one.

He nods and claps his hands together once in front of him. "All righty then, Caity-bug. Teach me."

The next half hour flies by in a blur of integral calculus and rates of change, our heads crowded close together as I explain different concepts to him. Noah nods along when he understands something and asks questions when he doesn't. He's a tutoring dream, never once complaining about anything and always ready and eager to learn. I'll miss helping him with math as much as I'll miss his friendship when he goes off to college. He'll be at UC San Jose, though, and that's only two hours from where we are now in Sacramento, so we could still see each other. I'm so glad he isn't going further than that. The idea of him being so far away would be too much to bear.

We finish our session and start packing our things. My eyes flick up at the clock and see that the bell will ring soon. If I'm going to give him the letter, it's now or never. Peeking over at Noah, I study him as he puts his papers away. He's so handsome, friendly, and sweet. Is it ridiculous of me to think he might like me too? As I slip the envelope out from under my folder and smooth it one last time, I really hope not. "Um, Noah?"

He glances up at me as he shuts his binder and stuffs it into his backpack. "What's up, Caity-bug?"

"Um." My teeth dig into the fragile skin of my bottom lip for a minute until Noah reaches over and pulls it free, shaking his head. I stare at him in shock, my lips tingling where his fingers brushed against them. By the rocked expression on Noah's face, I can tell that even he is a little surprised that he did that. Did he feel the same spark I did when we touched? Shaking off my surprise, I take a deep breath and keep my eye on the prize. This is my chance to be bold, and I don't want to miss it. "Um, I know you're graduating in a few weeks, and I wanted to..." I exhale shakily, so nervous that I can feel my heart beating a mile a minute and my palms begin to sweat. "Uh, I wanted to give you this." My hands tremble as I slide the envelope simply addressed with his first name in my loopy writing across the table. He glances down at it and quirks a brow at me before he picks it up.

As he turns the letter over in his hands, he asks, "Did you want me to read this now? Or later?"

"Now," I reply before I can change my mind. "Please?"

A small smile spreads over his face as he opens the envelope and pulls out the letter that details all my love and affection for him. I spent so long writing it that I know the words by heart:

Noah, I've been trying for days, weeks really, to think of the right words to tell you how I feel about you. If only there were tutors for writing love letters, right? But since there aren't, I'll just have to hope that what I came up with will do. Noah, I love you. You are the kindest, funniest, most caring and attentive person I have ever met. I love that we can talk about anything and that you listen to what I have to say without judgement. I love that we have a lot in common and can laugh at our never-ending argument over who would win in a fight: Batman or Iron Man. I love that you look past what other people don't bother to when it comes to me. You see past the big hair, glasses, and the stack of books I'm always carrying to the real me, the me who loves to laugh and be silly as well as serious and thoughtful. You are the first and only person to ever really be a friend to me, and I will always be grateful for that, whether or not you return my feelings. I know you're leaving for college, but I hope you know my love will go with you, and should you want to, we can still try to be together even though there will be a greater distance between us. I know you could have anyone in the world, but I hope you'll choose me. I love you so much, Noah Hunter, and I always will. Love, your Caity-bug.

I watch him intently, my breath held in my lungs as he reads through the words I took from my heart and wrote on the page. When he looks up, I can see some feeling flash across his face, but it's difficult to decipher. Was it love? I hope that's what I saw. I swallow thickly, emotion threatening to bubble to the surface, and bite on my lip to hold it in and try not to think the worst. Maybe he's just processing everything. He starts to open his mouth to speak, but before he can his football buddies come into the library and come toward our table.

"Hey, Hunter. We're busting you out of this geek shack. C'mon." His friend looks over at me and snorts dismissively before turning toward the door.

Noah stands up and grabs his things, the letter still clutched in his hands. "We'll talk later, okay?" he says quickly before heading for the door and his group of friends.

"Okay," I say quietly to no one. Well, that didn't go as I'd hoped, but maybe he just felt uncomfortable talking in front of his friends. Gathering my own things, I start walking to my first period history class, my chest tight with nerves and fear. There only one thing keeping my feet moving, the hope that everything between Noah and I will be cleared up later.

****

The bell for lunch rings and I grab my heavy backpack before heading to the lawn outside the cafeteria. Since we only get about twenty-five minutes to eat, I always bring my lunch so that I don't waste time in line for food. Finding my usual spot under the shade of a blue oak tree, I pull out my peanut butter sandwich. As I start picking at it, my mind once again focuses on what happened this morning and I wonder if Noah will try to find me after school. We don't have the same lunch period, so we can't talk now. Waiting to hear his thoughts on my letter is torture. I keep going back and forth between elation at the prospect of him returning my feelings and dread at how I'll repair the damage to my heart if he doesn't. As I chew on a bite of sandwich, a group of cheerleaders walks by and starts laughing. I look around to see what could be so funny, only to realize they're laughing at me. My hand brushes across my mouth, making sure I don't have something on my face when one of them says, "She wrote it all in a letter, can you believe it?" They start cackling again as they walk away. The sandwich turns to ash in my mouth and what little I got down sinks like a rock in my stomach, so I set the rest aside. *They're probably talking about someone else*, I tell myself. The thought gives me little comfort and my stomach continues to knot with worry as the lunch period passes by.

The sinking feeling I had at lunch gets worse as the afternoon goes on. I feel eyes on me in the hallways and I hear whispering in my classes. I wish I could tell myself that I'm just being paranoid, but I've gotten pretty good at being able to tell when people are talking about me. My parents do it all the time when they think I'm not listening, so it's become a bit of a sixth sense. After the last period bell rings, I grab my stuff and rush toward the parking lot, hoping to catch Noah and clear up all the confusion from the day. I'm sure Noah will explain everything when I see him. As I wait, I pace just inside the school gates, sweet relief flooding my body and calming my frayed nerves when I hear Noah's voice. I look up with a smile only to have it immediately drop off my face. Noah isn't alone, he's walking with his football buddies, and when his eyes find mine, they quickly dart away. My heart sinks at his lack of eye contact. That can't be good.

"Look, Noah. It's your Caity-bug. The one who hopes you'll choose her over everyone else," Noah's friend Cole says mockingly, punching him in the shoulder before he continues. "Why pick any of the hot cheerleaders who throw themselves at you when you could have a comic-loving nerd with big hair and glasses?" He sneers at me before laughing with his other friends.

My throat tightens as a lump forms there. If I was hoping the humiliation I just endured would end with Cole, that hope was in vain. Each of Noah's buddies takes a turn using my own words against me—talking about how I have no friends and that it was sad that I was so desperate to try and make something happen with Noah. My eyes well with tears until I can't take it anymore. I was hoping Noah would stand up for me—for us and our friendship at the very least—but he is eerily quiet. He doesn't join their mockery, but he doesn't stop it either. I can't believe he showed my letter to them. I gave him my heart and instead of rejecting me politely, he tossed it away like garbage. No, worse than that, he put it on display for the whole world to mock. Desperately hoping he'll finally do the right thing, I look at Noah one last time only to see that he can't meet my eyes. The tears that have been threatening all day finally spill over, and I turn tail and run the other way. Mercifully, I get to the girls' restroom in time to collapse in a stall as the tears flow down my face in earnest and gut-wrenching sobs, causing me to double over in pain for who knows how long.

Once the crying has finally stopped, I blow my nose and pull myself together as much as possible. As I exit the stall, I catch a glimpse of myself in the mirror. My eyes are bloodshot and my face is puffy. I look like I got hit by a train and I feel about just as good. Leaving the bathroom, I thank my lucky stars the campus is now empty and there are no more witnesses to the indignity I just suffered. As I make my way home, I spend the ten-minute walk thinking about what happened and how I'll have to face it all again on Monday. There's a little less than a month left of school, but the idea of spending that time getting mocked and having to see the person I love who did nothing to stop it makes me physically ill. I still can't believe Noah did that. If he didn't love me the way I love him, it would have hurt, but I would have gotten over it eventually I'm sure. But this? I thought we were friends, but no one would treat a friend the way he treated me today. He's clearly not the person I thought he was. The thought of being apart from him used to be unbearable, but right now, no distance is far enough to heal the hurt he caused. I could forgive him not loving me, but I don't know if I'll ever be able to forgive him for what happened today.

Chapter Two
Noah

Present Day

My sneakers slap against the pavement as I jog along the streets of the neighborhood adjacent to my apartment complex, my heart beating rhythmically with the sound. I came out early this morning to get ahead of the heat, but the longer I'm out the more I regret not sleeping in. It's summer in central California, so the heat is nothing to mess with. It doesn't compare to the blazing summers I faced as a youth down in Texas, but still, it's barely seven and I am covered in sweat. I didn't bother with a shirt today and I can feel the drops of moisture as they trail down my neck, back, and chest. Wiping my forehead with the back of my hand, I turn down the music pouring into my earbuds. My pace slows, along with my breathing, as I approach the parking lot near my apartment. I slow my steps even more until I am at a brisk walk, cooling myself down before I head inside.

A ping hits my ears and I grab my phone from the pocket of my jogging shorts. I slide it open and am greeted with a text from my father.

Dad: **Sent a package about a week ago. Some of your old stuff. Rams are looking good this pre-season.**

My eyes practically roll all the way into my head at his message. When he does call or text me, which, granted, is not very often, he always has to throw in something about football. When the college teams aren't playing, it's about the pros, and since neither are playing right now, it's all about training camps and how the teams are looking. I guess he's a Rams guy now since he's currently residing in Los Angeles.

My reply is nothing more than a simple thumbs-up, and I put my phone back in my pocket before making my way over to the mailboxes. Grabbing my keys, I open the box, finding another key for the package center. It's like a treasure hunt for what will most likely be useless crap I forgot to take with me from way back in the day. I'm honestly surprised he didn't just chuck the stuff in the garbage. My dad and I aren't close, so I'm wondering why he even bothered to go to the post office and send me something. I'll get my answer soon enough as I grab the small rectangular box and head over to my apartment. As I open the door, a cool breeze coming from the air conditioner hits my overheated, sweat-soaked skin causing me to shiver. It feels good after spending so much time in the warmth outside, and I drop my phone, keys, and the package on the kitchen counter. I grab myself a glass of ice water, rubbing it over my forehead before guzzling it down.

Once I've rehydrated, I grab a protein shake and down it on my way back to the bedroom. After a quick shower and change of clothes, I'm heading out to the family room once again, nabbing the package off the counter. Once I'm seated on the couch, I stare at the unremarkable brown box in my hands. Even though I'm sure it's nothing special, the curiosity of what's inside is eating away at me, and I tear off the packing paper, eager to see what lies beneath. When I see the top of the pile of papers and photos inside, I understand why my dad sent these to me instead of throwing them away. Sitting in the box is a stack of yellowing papers congratulating me on lettering in football from Washington High School in Sacramento. I huff a breath and remove it to see what's underneath only to find more football letters and team photos. I would have been fine to never see this stuff again, reminders from a time when I wasn't the best guy in the world. But I know why Dad sent them to me.

Football has always been in my life. Growing up in Franklin, Texas, football was king, and the one sport my dad cared about. He played on his high school football team and loved the sport, a little too much if you ask me. He's obsessed with the game and always has been. He sells insurance now, but he always loved football and wasn't happy that he wasn't good enough to play in college, though "not happy" is putting it mildly. I don't think he's ever gotten over it, and it made him bitter and resentful. It certainly didn't help that my mom got pregnant their senior year of high school. My dad and mom were high school sweethearts and when she got pregnant, they married and Dad got a job selling insurance with the help of his dad's friend. It didn't take long for the two of them to start resenting one another. My dad was mad that he had to support a family on top of missing out on a football career, and my mom was upset that she had to settle for a lowly insurance salesman. When I was about nine, my mom had enough and left without looking back. I don't blame her for leaving since my dad was a miserable man to live with, but I do blame her for leaving without me. She and I don't talk much now.

After she left, my dad didn't change and instead of resenting my mom, he resented me. The only time he managed to be a somewhat decent parent was when I was old enough to join the junior high football team. I showed a natural talent for the game and with my dad and I finally having something to bond over, he became marginally more bearable. Despite his constant criticism of my skills and need to train harder, he couldn't damper my own love for the game and we coexisted peacefully for the most part. That didn't last long, though. Dad got an offer to move around for work and decided that was the best way to see the world. We moved a good amount and I had a hard time making friends because of it. I always had football, though, and when we finally landed in Sacramento, I had a group of real friends at last. At least, that's what I thought at the time. As the quarterback of the football team, I was looked up to by my fellow teammates and had plenty of attention from the girls as well, but I didn't realize until later that it was just for show. They liked the status that came with being a part of my so-called entourage, not really caring about the person beyond the quarterback.

Our team made it to the state finals during my senior year. We didn't win, but my performance that day and the rest of the season as quarterback earned me a scholarship to UC San Jose. I played there for three years before I blew out my shoulder during pre-season. Luckily, I had already majored in secondary education with a minor in athletic training, so the injury didn't derail my own post-college career plans. I never banked on playing in the NFL and always enjoyed the idea of being a gym coach or athletic trainer for young kids, determined to make the high school experience better for them than it was for me by creating a sense of stability for the students. Luckily, after two years of teaching in San Jose, a spot for a gym teacher and football coach opened in Sun Valley and I took it. The school is small and they were all too happy to have a former college athlete as their new coach. I've been here ever since and I while I like it, there's something missing that doesn't make the small town feel quite like home.

Shaking off the melancholy that comes along with that thought, I refocus and move through the pile. Sifting through the pictures and notes from my "glory days" should fill me with pride and nostalgia, but all I feel is shame for the way I acted back then, thinking I was such hot stuff and passing on what I would come to realize later was probably one of the few chances I would have at real happiness with another person. It's not the first time I've berated myself for being such a fool back then and it probably won't be the last.

As if my thoughts about my past behavior conjured up some kind of magic, I set aside the last paper and see a rumpled envelope. I remember keeping the letter, *her* letter, but in all my moves since high school, I lost track of it. My name is written on the front in the loopy handwriting of the very same person I was just thinking about: Caitlin Walsh. The girl who spent hours tutoring me in math and became my only real friend in high school, not that I recognized it at the time. She didn't fawn over me and treat me like some big athletic star like everyone else did. I don't even think she knew a thing about football, but she knew so much about everything else. Math, books, comics—you name it, she had an opinion or idea about it. I used to love teasing her about her obsession with Batman, and she would give as good as she got, always chirping at me about how terrible the Fantastic Four movies were. I loved every minute I spent with her.

With shaky hands, I pick up the envelope and take out the letter. I haven't seen it in years, but I remember every word. She may as well have written it directly onto my heart because it's always stayed with me despite how horribly I acted toward her. As I stare down at the folded page, I think back on the girl who wrote it. Caitlin was the sweetest little thing. She was shy with just about everyone, but she opened up to me and I reciprocated, reveling in the way she would hang on my every word like I was spouting Shakespeare. She had a mass of red curls and thick glasses, but they framed an adorable face and outlined her shining green eyes. She might not have been considered as conventionally attractive as some of the other girls at school, but I still thought she was beautiful. Her kindness and sincerity shined through in everything she did, making her one of the most amazing girls to have ever crossed my path.

I unfold the letter and reread the words that she so bravely put down for me. She loved me, and while we didn't ever go out on an actual date, I believe she did have genuine feelings for me. I told her things I never told my "real" friends or anyone else for that matter. She knew that I moved around a lot as a kid and how much I hated it, and I knew about her too. She shared more with me than probably anyone else at school—how she always felt like she didn't belong, even in her own family, and how friends were hard to come by. I really liked her, though, and cherished her friendship. In fact, I was planning on asking her out on a date, but my friends caught me mooning over her letter during our first period class and snatched it right out of my hands. They teased me about it, and like a coward, I denied my feelings for her. That would have been bad enough, but they spread the story around the school and later that day, they mocked Caitlin to her face and I didn't do a damn thing about it, just stood there like an asshole and watched her heart break as they taunted her. I couldn't even bring myself to look at her while it happened. When I did catch a glimpse of her tear-stained face, twisted with misery as she ran from the scene, my heart broke for her and for what might have been. For as long as I live, I will never forgive myself for causing her that much pain.

Feeling like the worst kind of person, I tried to make it right, but no one knew where I could find her. I even went so far as to ask the front office for her home address, but they said they couldn't give out that information. I looked for her that following Monday at school, but she wasn't there and she never came back. Desperate for any scrape of information about her, I asked around and heard from the librarian that she was finishing the rest of the year at home, and I couldn't blame her. I wouldn't want to come back and face me either after the way I had treated her. Even if I had found her, I doubt she would have forgiven me. It's been eleven years and I still haven't forgiven myself.

Sniffing, I fold the letter back up and put it in the envelope. I go to set it in the pile with the rest of the memorabilia I plan on tossing, but I stop myself. This is proof that at one time someone thought I was worth loving. Maybe it's a sign as well. I tap the envelope against my thigh and grab my phone, opening my social media apps and typing in Caitlin's name. As I search the various profiles, my heart sinks when I don't see anyone who resembles my Caity-bug. After a good twenty minutes of searching, I toss my phone on the couch and rake my hands through my hair. If I thought the letter was a sign, maybe it was telling me I blew my one shot and wouldn't get another, at least not with her. Standing, I take the letter to my nightstand and carefully place it inside. I may not get my second chance, but I'm not ready to part with the letter just yet. It's a nice reminder to try and be a better man.

My phone dings and for one fleeting moment, I wonder if it's Caity somehow. Logically, I know that isn't possible, but hope rises in my chest and my heart races a bit anyway. I slide it open and see an invitation from Owen to grab a beer later this week. I reply in the affirmative before collapsing on my bed with a sigh. I may not get my second chance with Caity, but I'm not ready to give up hope just yet. I got my letter back, so maybe, just maybe, I'll get the girl back too.

Chapter Three
Caitlin

The last of the moving boxes has been filled with my gran's old things and I move it to the garage with the rest of the items destined for the landfill. It will take me about a dozen different trips in my little electric hybrid, but I'm putting that off for another day. As I dust my hands off on my cutoff shorts, I head back inside the one-story home my grandmother left to me in her will last year. My heart twinges as I miss my gran. She was one of the few people who seemed to understand me. She encouraged and supported my love of reading and supplied me with plenty of books, as many as I could handle. Gran was the best, and I wish I had spent more time with her before she passed.

My parents never really understood me as a person. They have always been concerned with appearances, status, and those things were never important to me. Because of that, I could never quite live up to their standards. From a young age, my head was always in a book and I shied away from all the activities they tried to get me involved in. With my clumsy ways, dance class was a disaster and I had zero aptitude for music, so piano lessons were another big waste of time. I was smart, so that pleased them, but I didn't use my intelligence to get involved in student government or speech and debate, so again, I fell short of where they wanted me to be. Once my younger brother was born, they pretty much gave up on me and I was left to my own devices.

The one nice thing they did was let me finish my junior year at home after the whole Noah Hunter debacle.

I don't want to relive that, though, so I shake away the memories that threaten to resurface and head over to the kitchen to start dinner. Glancing around the celery-green painted walls and old linoleum, I groan internally. This house is in major need of an update. It still looks almost exactly like it did when I first came here as a child, and if I have any chance of flipping it, which is probably the smartest course of action, I better start fixing it up. I'm not sure what I will do when I sell it. I've been in Northern California my whole life, having only moved from Sacramento to San Francisco for college, and now I'm here in Sun Valley. I should probably expand my horizons and explore the rest of the country, or even the world. Maybe I could find some beautiful library in Europe to work at and fall in love with some wonderful foreigner who would never betray my feelings.

That last part is probably wishful thinking, at least for me. My trust issues seem to ruin any relationship I try to have, not that there have been many. Instead of going down a shame spiral about my lack of a love life, I focus on dinner. Peeking inside the refrigerator provides a nice blast of cool air which feels refreshing after all the moving I've done. Too bad there isn't any food inside to reward myself with. I sigh and close the door before grabbing my phone and ordering food from Stop, Wok, and Roll, the tasty Asian cuisine shop down the street from my house. After requesting my favorites, I hang up and decide the best way to spend the wait is to plop myself onto the sofa and turn on a show. Whipping my frizz-filled hair into a bun, I grab the remote and search through my streaming service, stopping when I find an episode of *Sherlock*. The mystery holds my attention for a little while, but eventually my mind wanders back to my earlier thoughts.

It's not the first time I think back on what

happened in high school with Noah, but it's been a while. I said in the letter that I would always love him and I meant it at the time, but I think I was fooling myself. If the way he treated me the day I gave him my letter was any indication, he wasn't the person I thought he was, and how can you love someone when you don't really know them? Ugh, I hate that I keep coming back to this one stupid moment from over a decade ago. Anytime I think about my love life, I always come back to that one day, that one boy. I'm saved from ruminating on my thoughts any further when the doorbell rings and I get off the couch to retrieve my dinner.

After tipping the delivery person, I flop back onto the couch and dig into my beef and broccoli. I hit "play" on the show and watch as I eat my dinner. It's delicious and the show is as entertaining as always, but I wish I was watching it with someone. The couch is too big for one person, and dinner and a show isn't as much fun when you're always doing it solo. I've gotten better at socializing since my high school days, but I'm still not great at making the first step when it comes to friendships. My colleagues at the library in the city were great, but we didn't have much in common beyond our shared love of books. Maybe I'll make some friends at my new job but would settle for finding at least one other person to bond with. I still can't believe that come next week, I'll be the new librarian at Central High School. Being back in a high school environment isn't exactly ideal for me, but it was the only job available. I'm lucky I got the job when I did, otherwise I would have had to try and work on the house from over an hour away.

After finishing my dinner and the episode, I take my food containers into the kitchen and clean up. As my eyes roam around at the retro style of the flooring and cupboards, another sigh escapes me. I definitely have my work cut out for me with this place. Exhausted from an already busy day, I head up to bed and vow to get an early start in the morning. If I'm lucky, maybe I can get the garden in the back replanted before the beginning of the school year.

****

The garden replanting goes a little better than expected, and the purple and white blooms on the petunias look wonderful in the light of the late evening sun. It's still hot as heck outside, but I've moved into the shade of the porch and am cooling off with a nice glass of lemonade. My finger runs down the side of the glass gathering the condensation as it sits on the patio table. I move my gaze from the water droplets and let it roam around the backyard. The mature trees provide a good amount of shade, and the grass is in pretty good shape after I had a company put down some new sod at the beginning of the summer. This would be a great backyard for kids to play in. Allowing myself to daydream a little, I close my eyes and picture a young boy on a tire swing hanging from the big tree in the corner. His little sister is twirling in the grass, her dress fanning out as she goes around and around in circles. A smile pulls at my face as I imagine warm lips grazing my cheek as my husband sits down next to me. In my mind, I gaze over at him and peer into his gorgeous hazel eyes, getting lost in their depths for a moment before I lean over to run my fingers through his silky, brown locks.

Abruptly, I snap out of my daydream and bolt upright in my chair. I know those hazel eyes and that brown hair. I still occasionally dream about them at night and I want to slap myself for going there yet again. It's bad enough that Noah Hunter occasionally finds his way into my dreams while I sleep, but now he's invaded my daydreams too. Berating myself for being so stupid, I stand up and walk inside the house, trying to escape the images from the backyard that were all too tempting. I don't want them to be real. I don't. *I don't, I don't, I don't,* I chant over and over in my head. Maybe if I say it enough times, it will be true.

I walk into my bedroom and pace back and forth, wearing down the already threadbare carpet. Needing to get this man out of my system once and for all, I go to the closet and pull out a box with all my old high school stuff, sifting through the report cards and old letters of recommendation from teachers until I find what I am looking for: the newspaper clipping from the *Sacramento Bee*, the local paper. It's from my junior year, the year the football team went to state. The paper did an article on the teams and even though ours didn't win, somehow a picture of our quarterback ended up next to it. I stare at the old photo of Noah, my heart thumping in my chest as I'm transported back to another time, a time when I thought I loved him and he might return the feelings. His helmet is off and his hair is sweaty and disheveled, but he still looks as gorgeous as he always did. Even in the black-and-white photograph, I can see his eyes sparkling with the same humor and mischief I remember.

My fingers run over the image and I sniffle. How can I still be so affected by this guy? I take one final moment to appreciate what he was to me at one point in time: a friend. My only friend. H didn't treat me well in the end, though, and all I'm left with is the memory of that pain and this picture. Resolved to finally be free of the past, I raise it up to tear it in two, but as I bring it to my face, I find that I can't do it. A part of me still can't bear the thought of destroying the last tangible reminder I have of him. I sigh and put the paper back in the box, closing the lid. I'm disappointed in myself to be honest. I've tried hard to get over the past, but clearly a part of me is still stuck there on that day with the boy I loved so much. Shoving the box in the back of the closet before shutting the door, I rest my forehead against the hard wood and try to calm myself. I can close the door on the picture from my past, but I can't seem to close the door on the feelings I had. Turning to leave, I glance back at the closet one last time. I may not be able to close the door on those feelings, but at least for the time being, I can walk away from them.

Chapter Four
Noah

The evening light filters in from the windows and gives The Greedy Goat a soft glow. I glimpse the light-green walls of the pub decorated with various photographs and paintings as I walk toward the bar where I can already spot my best friend, Owen Graham. As I approach, I slap him on the back to announce my presence. "How's it going, man?"

He turns and has a dopey, love-struck look on his face, the same look that's been there ever since he and his other best friend, Madeline, got together a couple of months ago. It's gotten even worse since they got married last week at the courthouse. "It's going great! I can't believe I waited so long to be with Madi. What was I thinking?"

I chuckle because I don't think anyone can believe the two of them waited nine years to get together. It was a constant source of irritation for me and Owen's sister. Then again, since I haven't ever really been in a serious relationship, I guess I can't give him too hard a time. I clear that thought out of my head and get back to my friend. "I'm surprised you wanted to meet, actually. I figured y'all would still be on your honeymoon."

"Oh, we don't have to be in another city to still be on our honeymoon," he says with a comical waggle of his eyebrows. The man has been incorrigible since he started getting laid regularly and I would be irritated if I weren't so damn happy for him.

Still, I shove him and he almost falls off his stool. "Dork." He tries to shove me back, but I don't budge. As a physical education teacher and the varsity football coach, I take my health and fitness seriously and I enjoy working out quite regularly, so I'm basically a wall of muscle. Even though Owen is no slouch and is fairly built himself, he's no match for me.

"Jeez, dude. Lighten up on the exercise. You're making the rest of us look bad," Owen tells me with a furrowed brow.

"Nah, I'm just making myself look extra good." I jokingly flex my muscles to illustrate.

Owen rolls his eyes and I don't blame him. I've gotten pretty good at playing up my vanity, but he knows it's all for laughs. "Anyway," he starts, "I wanted to meet up because it's been a while. I've been caught up with Madi and I didn't want you to think our friendship didn't matter anymore now that I'm married."

"Well, I appreciate that, but I didn't think you forgot about me. Hell, I wouldn't blame you for pulling a disappearing act now that you finally got your girl." I'm sure that's how I would be if I ever found anyone that wanted to be with me for more than one night. An image of red curls and green eyes flashes through my mind and I shove down the pain that always follows anytime I think of Caitlin Walsh. It's been happening a lot lately, ever since I uncovered that letter she gave me all those years back. I did have someone who wanted me, all of me, forever, and I wanted her just as much. I was a fool for not grabbing onto her with both hands and never letting go, a mistake I won't repeat the next time that kind of love comes my way. If it ever does.

"It's tempting, believe me," he admits. "But Madi needed some girl time with Amelia and I thought I would take the opportunity to catch up with you."

"Where's Gabe?" Gabriel Hernandez is our other friend and is engaged to Owen's sister, Amelia. He joined our little friend group when he started his position as vice principal at Central High School last year. He's a great guy and I'm glad he stepped outside his comfort zone to get to know us. I'll never say no to a new friend.

"I asked him to come out, but he's doing a few things around the house for his mom. Truthfully, though, I just think he wanted to be closer to the apartment in case Amelia called." Ever since they found out Amelia's pregnant, Gabe's been even more attentive to his fiancée and hasn't wanted to leave her side. It's interesting to see a guy who was so against relationships be totally committed to his girl and their baby.

"Well, I guess it's a good thing I'm about to be busy with the football season. I won't have time to miss my friends," I lament. Truth be told, I don't love being alone. It gives me too much time to think back on past wrongs I've committed and the regrets I have.

"How is the team shaping up this year, by the way?"

The question is a welcome distraction from my maudlin thoughts, and I slap my hand on Owen's back, a smile pulling across my face. "They're actually lookin' really good. I reckon we have an actual shot at regionals this year." I don't need to get far for myself, but I know how hard my boys work and it will be nice if it pays off this year.

"That's great, man," Owen says with a grin. "I know you've put in a lot of hard work with the team."

"Yeah, I put in the work, but so do they." I see Arthur Graham, Owen's dad and owner of the pub, walking up to us. "Hey there, Arthur."

"Hello, Noah. Good to see you out and about." He looks to his son. "Owen, my boy! Your lovely wife sick of you already?" The older man smiles and his eyes crinkle in the corner. He's always giving Owen a hard time, something I find endlessly entertaining, and I have to hold in my laughter.

"Hardy-har-har, Dad." Owen goes to playfully punch his father, but Arthur is too fast and ducks it.

"I'm just messing with you, kiddo," he says with a wink. "Now, how about I go grab a couple of pints and a basket of chips for you two?"

"Sounds great! Thanks, Arthur." The fries here are the best around and always brighten my mood. I smile kindly at the elder Graham and turn back to my friend. "So, you ready for the school year?"

"Aren't I always?" Owen is one of the smartest guys I know, so it's no surprise that he's already ready and rarin' to go. "You?"

"I think I'm good as far as classes go. I do think I'll be spending most of my free time putting together plays for the team, though." Not that I mind. With my friends all shacked up and my quitting dating apps months ago, I've been a little bored. There's only so much Netflix and exercising a man can take before he starts to lose his mind.

Arthur comes back and drops a couple of beers and a basket of fries in front of us. "Here you go, gentlemen." I pull out my wallet to cover the tab and Arthur waves it away. "You know your money's no good here, Noah."

"I appreciate that, Arthur. Thank you." He tips his head full of graying brown hair at me and as I watch him amble off to the other end of the bar, I see a tall blonde tip her glass at me with the clear intention of trying to start something. I nod politely and turn back to Owen to see that he's giving me a weird look. "What?" I can't help but ask.

"Nothing. It's just weird to see you turning down an obviously interested woman, that's all."

He's not wrong. It is a little unusual for me, at

least the old me. In high school and college, I was highly sought after as a single date or one-night stand, a story for girls to tell their friends, that they got with the quarterback. It didn't take long for me to see that's all they really wanted—a story. I didn't want to be the guy that slept around, and football really was my sole focus, so I just brushed off most offers and only hooked up when I felt the need. I figured I had my one shot with someone who loved me for who I was, not just what's on the outside or my football status, but I blew it big time, so I tried to have a little fun and not take things too seriously. It didn't used to bother me—only being the good-time guy—but something changed. I don't know if it's because my friends are all in relationships now or because I'm almost twenty-nine years old, but I want someone to see me for more than that. I ignore the ache in my chest as thoughts of my Caity-bug threaten to resurface. That ship sailed and I need to move past it.

Newly resolved, I slap my hand down on the bar. "Well, get used to it. I want something real and I'm not going to settle for a random hookup."

"You could always try for something real with her." Owen posits and nods his head in the direction of the blonde.

I take one look at the woman and from the sly smile on her face, I can tell she's not looking for more than a good time. "Nah, I couldn't. I know what real looks like and that woman isn't it." For years I was content to pass the time with random women, but not anymore. Now I want the real thing, and being with someone for just one night almost feels like cheating now. And one thing I am not and never have been is a cheater.

"Well, I hope you find the real thing soon, man." Owen claps my shoulder before taking a long pull of his beer. We start talking about other things as we continue to drink and munch on the fries, but my mind keeps drifting back to Caity and how much pain I caused her. Over ten years later and I still regret that day. I never got a chance to make things right, and more than anything, I wish I could have another shot with her. I have no idea how that would even be possible now. She's probably married with kids and everything, or she's super successful with all the male attention she could handle. Only an idiot would give up a chance with a girl like her. I just wish that idiot hadn't been me.

Chapter Five
Caitlin

The Central High School library smells like books and teenage angst. I know the scent all too well and being back in a school library is like taking a trip down memory lane. Not all the memories are good ones, but they aren't all bad either. I had some pretty good times in the library, escaping into other worlds that were so much nicer than my own, feeling like I had a place I could be my true self. My eyes roam around the room as I take in the cool gray walls and half shelves of books, making my way toward the office in the back. A chuckle escapes as I walk. I still can't believe I took a job at a high school.

The best part of my day in high school was when I tutored Noah Hunter, but even those memories are tainted with the way he so casually let his friends mock my love letter. I couldn't go back to school after that day. Once again I'm grateful to my parents for letting me finish the year at home. I told them I was being bullied and we all met with a school counselor, but when pushed for details I said nothing. I didn't want to go over the humiliating events again and even though Noah was a part of it, I didn't want him to get in trouble. I never saw him again after that day, and luckily for me, most of his buddies and followers graduated and weren't around my senior year. I got the occasional weird glance and heard odd whispers every now and then, but I held my head high and ignored them, focusing on school and getting into college.

Even though it held some painful memories, I still

loved the library at my high school and continued to tutor my final year there. After I graduated, I moved on to City College of San Francisco where I got my degree in library science. I didn't have many relationships while I was there, feeling distrustful of anyone who showed the slightest interest in me. Most of my time was spent in the library, as usual, and I couldn't think of a better place to work when I finished my schooling. After college graduation, I got a job at the San Francisco Public Library and worked there up until two months ago when I moved to Sun Valley. It had been a dream job, but my life there had grown stagnant, and when Gran left me her house, I saw it as an opportunity to shake things up.

The office door creaks as I head inside and look around. After placing my box on the empty desk, I start removing my personal belongings and arrange them to make the space a little more comfortable, starting with a couple of photographs. One picture is with my parents and my brother on the day of my college graduation, and the next is a picture of me with my city library friends on my last day of work. I look very different in the two photos. The first reflects how I looked for most of my youth, my red curls a little out of control and my black-rimmed glasses always askew. The second reflects how I look now after having discovered curl cream, a diffuser for my hair-dryer, and contact lenses. Glancing down at my current state of dress, you can tell I am still the quiet, nerdy girl I've always been. My outfit of the day consists of cutoff shorts and a Marvel comic t-shirt, but I like who I am now and don't hide as much as I used to. I still have a hard time making friends, but I'm getting better.

I smile as I take out the little potted succulent my ex-boyfriend gave me a couple of years ago. I met William in the city and we dated for a year, but things fizzled out after a while. We liked each other well enough, but I don't think we really loved one another. I was always a little too shy for him and he was always a little too flirtatious with other women for my liking. I was never really convinced he liked me, and that hurt our relationship too. I kept the succulent, though. It's in a cute little cat pot and it's the only plant I've managed to keep alive, probably because I barely have to water it, but still. My other items find a place in my new space: a Batman bobblehead, a mug covered in book spines, and a fuzzy blanket. Once I've made my little office as cozy as possible, I walk out to the shelves and think about getting started with the organizing and cleaning. There are a couple of weeks until school starts and I want to make the library look as welcoming and friendly as possible. I even have some ideas for decorating. Walking over to the large window, I gaze out onto the campus grounds, taking in the locker bays, small verandas, and grassy areas I can already picture students camping out on. I may be back on a high school campus, but I'm a different person now, so there's no need for me to be feeling afraid, even though there is a touch of that in my body right now. I tell myself it will settle eventually, and the excitement will take over. Besides, nothing could happen at this high school that could possibly compare to the awfulness I experienced at my last one.

****

As I stare in the mirror in the library bathroom, I analyze my appearance, looking for anything amiss. I'm wearing berry-colored capris, a flutter-sleeved, white floral blouse, and white kitten heels. My curls are looser today, so they hit about halfway down my torso. I don't normally wear much makeup, but I added some eyeshadow and mascara to my staple face powder and lip gloss routine. Since I will be introduced at the first professional development meeting of the school year, I put a little more effort into my look today. There are still a couple of days left before students arrive, but the teachers and staff are here early to set up. I've been here for a few weeks and met a couple of people already, and they all seem very friendly, but I'm still nervous. It's been a long time since I had to talk in front of a group of people who weren't all librarians and my chest flutters with a touch of anxiety.

Pushing my nerves aside for the moment, my finger runs through the wine-colored lip stain, and I reapply it gingerly before touching up the smoky eye shadow I put on earlier this morning. I had to watch a YouTube tutorial three times before I could get it right since I've never been good at makeup, but thank God for the Internet, even if watching the video over and over almost caused me to be late. Speaking of which, I should make my way over to the meeting. Fortunately, it's in the classroom at the back of the library, so it takes less than thirty seconds to get there. Quietly as possible, I slip in the side and see that the room is already mostly full. I grab a seat near the front and take out my notebook and a pen, ready to jot down any important information that may come my way.

After a few minutes, Principal Langley comes in the room and heads straight to the front. The older woman, along with two others, interviewed me for the job and she was very friendly and welcoming. When I look around, I spot the other two administrators I met at the interview. Mark Wilson was affable and seemed like a nice guy, and Gabriel Hernandez was nice as well, though more serious and focused than his two counterparts. He seems in good spirits today as he places his hand around the back of the chair occupied by a beautiful blonde woman. They look at each other lovingly and there's no doubt they're a couple. It's hard not to smile at their obvious love, and it answers the question of whether fraternizing with colleagues is allowed, not that I intend on getting involved with anyone romantically anytime soon.

Principal Langley clears her throat loudly, garnering the attention of everyone in the room. "Okay, people, let's get started. Welcome to another year at Central High School." She pauses and everyone claps. There are even a few yelps of joy thrown in for good measure. I belatedly join in, bringing my hands together, and I'm happy that everyone at least seems enthusiastic about the school year. It bodes well for how my own year will go if the staff are this excited. "Before we get into reviewing the latest policy changes, I'd like the new members of the staff to introduce themselves."

Okay, I guess it's good to get this over with at the beginning. I don't think I can hold my nerves for the entire meeting, but I'm still hoping that one of the other new staff members goes first so I don't have to think of what to say and can just copy them.

"Because we have such an amazing school and such little turnover, we only have one new staff member this year. You probably recall that Derek Lombardo retired last year so we have a new school librarian and media center coordinator, Caitlin Walsh. Caitlin, why don't you go ahead and say a little bit about yourself?"

Sharon Langley gestures for me to stand and I do so reluctantly. My legs tremble and I teeter slightly on my heels. I didn't know I would be the only person doing this and I can feel the sweat forming on my brow and upper lip at the thought of being singled out. I guess I better do this quickly before I melt off all my makeup. Exhaling a shaky breath, I turn around to face the room, swallow my nerves, and plaster a smile on my face.

"Um, hello, everyone." I start to wave, then quickly put my hand down because that seems silly and childish. "I'm Caitlin and I'm new to Sun Valley. I'm coming from the San Francisco Public Library, but I'm very familiar with high school libraries since I spent most of my time there when I was a teen." I hear a few chuckles and that eases some tension in my shoulders. "I'm very excited to get to know you all and am available to help with anything you might need for your students or your own lesson plans."

When I scan the room and see lots of smiling, friendly faces, I'm actually excited at the prospect of socializing with the staff. I start to turn back around when my eyes catch on a figure sitting in the back of the room. My mouth falls open as my eyes widen in disbelief. He's older now, his hair is shorter and a shade darker, and he has a good amount of stubble lining his jaw, but there is no mistaking that the man I am staring at is Noah Hunter. Noah, the boy I loved, the boy who broke my heart. He's staring directly back at me, and my mouth closes and pulls into a frown. What is he doing here? I didn't try to look him up at all after that day in high school. I was tempted to, so very tempted, but I didn't want to see how happy he was and how much losing my friendship didn't affect him in the slightest when it all but crushed me. We stare at each other a moment longer before I hear Sharon talking to me. "Was there more you wanted to say, Caitlin?"

I pull my gaze away from Noah and look at her, confused, before I realize I'm still standing in front of the room. "N-no, I'm good," I stammer out before I stumble back into my chair. I face the front, trying to slow my heartbeat and squelch the panic that is rising in my chest. Maybe I was seeing things. Maybe I got so nervous and being back in a high school made me imagine Noah. I have been thinking about him a lot lately. God, I should have torn up that stupid picture the other day. None of that would explain the change in his appearance, though, and I hazard a glance back to where he was sitting. When I peek over my shoulder, I see he's still staring at me with a look of disbelief on his handsome face. It's not fair that he still looks so beautiful after everything that happened. Couldn't he at least be bald or something? Where is karma when you need her? I'm still staring at him when a smile pulls across his face. How dare he smile at me? I furrow my brow and turn back toward the front of the room.

I tell myself I won't look back at Noah again, but I do at least half a dozen times and each time I do, he's smiling at me like everything is completely normal, fantastic even, like the entire universe didn't just flip over. The rest of the meeting goes by in a blur and I only half pay attention, thoughts spiraling about what to do and whether I can survive without the job I just started. It doesn't take more than a thought of my current bank account balance to realize that I can't. I need money to fix up the house and besides, I'm not going to let a little thing like seeing Noah Hunter stop me from doing what needs to be done. I'm not the same person I was in high school. I've grown, matured, and I can handle being in his presence, no problem. But as the meeting ends and the staff is dismissed, I sprint from my chair, not daring to stick around long enough to find out whether that's actually true.

Chapter Six
Noah

I only half listen as Principal Langley starts the meeting, and I join in absently as I hear the clapping to usher in a new school year. I'm too preoccupied with the gorgeous woman I see out of the corner of my eye to do anything more than that. Most of her face is hidden from me as she's sitting up front and is paying attention to what is going on, but her milky-white skin, scarlet red hair, and button nose are the only things I can concentrate on. Who is she, and why does she seem familiar? Maybe I saw her out one night, but I don't think so. I would definitely have remembered this woman. Hell, if I saw her out at a bar I would have approached her and bought her a drink at the very least. I'm still staring at the mystery woman when I hear Sharon Langley say two words I never thought I would hear spoken aloud again: Caitlin Walsh.

The rest of her talking turns into nothing but white noise because I'm too busy watching as the same woman I have been obsessing over for the last few minutes stands up and turns around. Now that I can see all of her, I can't believe I didn't put it together moments ago. Caitlin is still the same sweet girl I knew all those years ago. Her oval face looks the same and her smile is as bright and beautiful as it was back when we were friends. She's wearing contact lenses instead of the rimmed glasses and her hair is a little longer and the red curls she was always pushing out of her face are looser. I feel the need to run my fingers through them to see if they are as soft as they look.

"Um, hello everyone," I hear her say as she starts

to wave before self-consciously lowering her hand, acting as adorably awkward as she always did. Her voice is slightly deeper than it used to be with a slightly smokey quality to it, and I get so lost in the beautiful sound that I don't really hear the words. She mentions something about spending a lot of time in the library and a few people chuckle because they think it's a joke, but I know better. She did always spend her time in the library and I was there for a good chunk of that before I went and ruined everything. My eyes flick down to see her hands clasped tightly together and I frown at her anxiousness, wanting nothing more than to hug her so tightly that I squeeze all the tension from her little body. At least she's still smiling, and those straight, white teeth sparkle as she scans the room. When her gaze lands on me, though, the smile drops and she stands stock still, like a deer in headlights. I have no idea what she sees on my face, but I feel just as shocked as she looks.

Principal Langley asks if she has anything else to add and that snaps her out of her stupor, answering in the negative before hurriedly retaking her seat. The meeting progresses and as I look over at her, she's hiding her face from me, on purpose I'm sure, but every now and then, she'll glance back. I have no idea what is going on during the meeting because my mind is taken up with thoughts of my Caity-bug returning to me after all these years. A wide smile comes over my face when I realize what's happening. This isn't a coincidence, this is fate. Just as I got that letter back, just as I was wishing I could have another chance with Caitlin, she shows up as the new school librarian. I finally have a chance to make things right between us and hopefully I can convince her to give me a shot.

When Caitlin turns around to look at me again, I see her brows pull together and she frowns. She's not happy to see me, and I can't blame her. After that day eleven years ago, I wasn't able to find her to set things right. She didn't have many friends, so no one could give me her phone number or tell me where she lived. Fate didn't have my back then, but it has smiled upon me now and I'm going to take advantage. Caitlin turns around to the front and doesn't look at me again for the rest of the meeting. As soon as we are dismissed, she bolts out the door and into the main part of the library like there is hellfire at her feet. Luckily, my classroom is a gym and I have very little to do there, so I have all the time in the world to play cat and mouse.

I stand up and start to head out when Madi Graham stops me with a hand on my arm. "What's going on with you?" she asks, her expression concerned but also slightly accusatory.

I shrug my shoulder, playing dumb. I don't have time for twenty questions right now. "What do you mean? Nothing is going on with me. Now, there's somewhere I need to be, so if you don't mind…" I start to push my way past Owen's wife, but she stops me again, this time more forcefully. The tall brunette is intimidating on the best of days and most people cower before her. That's not the case for me, and while I could muscle my way past her, she's also a good friend and I don't want to disrespect her.

"I do mind. You had this weird look on your face during the meeting and couldn't stop staring at the new librarian. And don't think I didn't notice that she was looking back at you as well. What was that all about?"

Owen comes up and puts his arm around his wife. "Yeah, we noticed some weirdness going on. What's the story? Tinder date gone wrong?" he asks around a large mouthful of muffin, a few crumbs spraying from his mouth as he does.

I scowl at his joke. "Look, I'll tell y'all later. Right now there is somewhere I need to be." I turn around to go the other way when I run smack into Amelia. Fortunately, her fiancé is right behind her and catches her in his arms.

"Are you all right, *querida*?" Gabe asks her as his hand moves over the small swell of her baby bump.

She beams her bright smile at him and places her hand over his. "I will be once Noah spills about why he was eyeballing the new girl."

I growl in frustration. "Can I please just go? I don't need all of you in my business right now." I need to see my girl and get to making things right.

"You're in our business all the time and now you're in the hot seat, so spill it," Amelia demands. She pokes me in the chest for good measure with one of her pink fingernails.

"Ow, jeez, all right. Just put that away." I bat her hand away from my chest and rub at the sore spot. She pokes really hard and I remind myself not to piss off a pregnant Amelia again. "I will give y'all the CliffsNotes version and that's it for now, okay?" When they all agree to my terms, I give them a shortened version of the events that happened in high school. Even leaving out all the details, I don't come out looking great.

Amelia pokes my chest again. "How could you do that to her? That's messed up, Noah." She emphasizes how displeased she is by punctuating each word with another chest poke.

"Yeah, that's pretty messed up, dude," Owen agrees with his sister, and I don't argue against it. I deserve all the upset coming at me right now.

"I know and I wanted to make things right back then, but I wasn't able to. Now I can and would like to go about doing that, so if y'all would just get out of my way that would be great." I want to start making things up to Caitlin as soon as possible and being waylaid by my friends is putting that off.

They back up to give me room and Gabe claps my shoulder. "I'm just going to pretend you're working in the gym and not harassing the new employee." He grabs Amelia's hand and they make their way outside.

"Good luck, man." Owen and Madi follow the other two out the door and I'm left alone in the classroom. I look over at the door to the library, but I can't see much through the tiny window, so I'm not sure if Caitlin is still there or not. As I look down at my clothes, I grumble to myself. For the first time I wish my uniform consisted of more than track pants and a school t-shirt. Oh well, it will have to do. I run my hands through my hair as I approach the door, trying to smooth it out and look as presentable as possible. Taking a deep breath, I reach for the handle, not knowing what awaits me on the other side, but I'm hopeful that it could be the start of something wonderful.

After walking around and quickly scanning the bookshelves and computer area, I finally find Caitlin back in her office. I knock on the doorframe and she startles, dropping some papers to the floor. She bends down to pick them up and I go to help her. "I got it, it's fine," she says. She doesn't look up to see me until our fingers brush. The brief touch sends sparks of awareness up my arm and I can't help but reach for her.

I grasp her soft, delicate hand in mine and still her movements. "Hi, Caity-bug," I whisper. Her name feels so good on my lips and I want to say it to her reverently for as long as she'll let me.

Her eyes meet mine and they're the same stunning shade of emerald green. Without her glasses, I can see them more easily now and they are gorgeous. Staring into them feels like I've been punched in the gut with a force greater than anything else I have ever felt. Her eyes sparkle for a moment and there's a lightness there, but it fades quickly and is replaced by a slight sadness as she pulls her hand away. "D-don't call me that, please." She stands up and puts the papers on the desk before she starts fidgeting with the hem of her floral blouse, just like she used to in school and I would smile at the fact that I still make her nervous, but I know that until we clear the air, it will be for all the wrong reasons.

"What would you like me to call you then, darlin'?" I ask, hoping the softness in my voice will help stop her fretting.

She closes her eyes and pinches the bridge of her nose where I see a smattering of freckles. The desire to lean over and kiss each cinnamon-colored sprinkle is strong but ill-timed, so I resist. "I don't really know, Noah. I wasn't expecting to see you here."

"Yeah, I, uh, guessed as much by the look of horror on your face. You'd think I said that Superman was an overgrown Boy Scout or something." I smile and hope I can bait her with some of our old banter.

She doesn't go for it, though. She opens her eyes and crosses her arms over her middle, like she needs to protect herself from me, the action causing pain to slice through my chest. I never want her to be afraid of me. "What do you want, Noah?" she asks, her eyes weary.

You, I think to myself, but I can't say that to her, not yet. For all I know, she's married or has a boyfriend. I glance down at her left hand and don't see a ring, so at least I don't have that to worry about. I suppose the best way to go about this is to be as truthful as possible. "I want to explain, to make things right between us."

She scoffs. "You really think that's possible? Noah, I poured my heart out in that letter and you showed it to your friends like it was some kind of joke. I couldn't even face going back to school after all the laughing and taunting that day."

I see the pain in her eyes and I hate that I'm the cause of it, and while I wasn't exactly a saint, it wasn't quite as bad as she thinks. Did I break her heart and act like a complete jerk? Absolutely. But it wasn't my intention. A ball started rolling and I did nothing to stop it, but I can make things right now. I hold up my hands in supplication. "I know that day was awful for you and if I could go back in time and do it differently I would, believe me I would. I didn't mean for any of that to happen, but I didn't stop it either and for that I will forever be ashamed of myself."

I reach my hand out, palm facing up, and hold my breath as she eyes it skeptically. If I don't get the opportunity to explain myself, this will go nowhere fast. After what feels like an eternity, she uncrosses her arms and puts her hand in mine, the simple gesture feeling like a lot more than the olive branch it is. I finally breathe out before telling her my side of the story.

"I know you may not believe this, but I really liked your letter. It was the first time I felt like someone really liked me for who I was and not what I was—a football player. I didn't mean for those guys to get ahold of it, but they caught me reading it again during first period and took it from me. They razzed me about it pretty bad and..." I look up at the ceiling for a minute to gather the strength to admit this. "I denied that I had feelings for you when that couldn't have been further from the truth. You were a good friend to me and I betrayed that friendship by standing there and doing nothing while they mocked you." I look deep into the emerald jewels that are her eyes and squeeze her hand, hoping to convey just how much I regret my past actions.

"I hate myself for how stupid I was that day. I let the fact that I was Mr. Popular and finally had a group of friends prevent me from doing the right thing. I realized later that night what a terrible thing I had done. You were a better friend to me than those guys ever were. Hell, I didn't even talk to them again after graduation, so what was it all for really? To save face in front of a group of jerks?" I scoff. "If I had a time machine, I'd go back and kick my own ass for how I acted."

That earns me a small smile and I take it as a sign to continue. "I tried to make things right with you, Caity-bu … Caitlin, but you didn't come back to school and I didn't have your phone number. I was ready to go to your house to apologize, but no one knew where you lived and after a few weeks, I was off to training camp for college ball and figured I had lost my chance." I rub my thumb over her knuckles.

She looks down at our hands and then back up to me. There are tears in her eyes and I hope I didn't just make things worse. She sniffs and blinks away the moisture that threatened to spill out over her face. "Is that all?"

I pull back a little. "Um, yeah, that's it." Her hand falls from mine and she turns around and starts messing with the papers on her desk. "So, you accept my apology?"

"Was that an apology? Funny, I don't remember hearing the words, 'I'm sorry.' All I heard was that you feel bad about not being a better person and now you're here to make yourself feel better about that one time you were a jerk to the class nerd."

My brow furrows as I realize I'm not doing this right. "Caitlin, I am sorry. I should have started out with that, but please know that I truly am and it's not just because I want to make myself feel better. I want us to get to know each other again, to start over." I thought she would be more receptive to me, but I guess I underestimated just how badly I hurt her.

She turns around and sighs. "Do you know why you couldn't get my number or find my house? It's because you were my only friend, Noah, or at least that's what I thought. If we really were friends, though, you would have had both of those. We would have hung out away from the library and would have texted on the phone like other friends do, but that's not what we were and I deluded myself into thinking I was more to you than just a tutor." She dashes away a rogue tear and crosses her arms again. "Now, I will help you out in a helpful librarian capacity if you should require it, but you don't need to feel like you owe me anything beyond professional courtesy. You apologized and I accept that you feel sorry for what you did, but you broke my heart, badly," she says, her voice cracking. "That's not something I can just forget after one conversation."

I nod and process everything she's just said, knowing I need to make more of an effort to show her I'm not the guy I was back then, and I will do that. I look into her eyes again, willing her to believe what I'm about to say. "Thank you for accepting my apology, but I want you to know that I'm not giving up on us. I'm going to convince you that I'm the man you thought I was, Caitlin Walsh, the man from the letter you wrote who was deserving of your love and attention. Don't give up on me." It takes every effort to pull my gaze from her and leave the office, but I manage it, heading out of the library toward the gym with ideas of how to win back my Caity-bug spinning through my mind. I don't care what it takes or how much effort I need to put in. I've got my second shot, and I'm not going to waste it.

Chapter Seven
Caitlin

My heart clenches as I watch Noah leave the library from the window of my office. Did that really just happen? I'm still reeling from his confession—that his friends took my letter from him. He still stood by and did nothing to stop their bullying, but I remember him talking about moving around a lot growing up. He never felt like he belonged anywhere until he came to our school, so can I really blame him for not wanting to give that up when he finally found it?

Ugh, I'm so confused. He broke my heart back then and even though I understand the motivations for his actions now, it doesn't change what happened. I still carry the scars of that day with me. In the years that followed, I could never trust that a guy might actually like me. I had a string of less-than-stellar dates and hookups before I met William, and even that didn't last. I can't blame that all on Noah, though. My self-esteem was never great, and while I like who I am, those old doubts still resurface now and again, and I'm still awkward around others until I get to know them better. I shake my head to try and clear all the complicated thoughts from my head. I need to concentrate on this new job and fixing up Gran's old house, not on Noah and his promise to make things right between us.

I'm not sure what he really means by that anyway, and I don't want to think about it too much or I could be in danger of getting my hopes up. Noah Hunter is still as devastatingly handsome as he was in high school, more so because he now has the look and swagger of a confident, adult man and not just an arrogant boy. His hair is shorter than it was in high school, but I like that I can see more of his heart-shaped face and hazel eyes. I tried not to stare into them as he spoke to me, but he looked at me so intently that it was impossible not to. There are little flecks of green and blue near the pupils and the iris seems to be lined with a slight gold ring. I don't think I noticed that much detail before. I guess I was too taken up with how wonderfully he treated me when we were together to notice.

I definitely noticed his body in high school, and did again today. He was always athletic—as a quarterback, he had to be in shape, but he was lither and leaner back then. The t-shirt he wore today stretched across his taut torso, the sleeves struggling to contain his bulging biceps, and I hate myself for wondering what they would feel like wrapped around me. I mentally slap myself. *That way lies madness, Cait.* Noah Hunter didn't want me then and despite everything he just said, I highly doubt he would want me now. This is just a way to assuage the guilt he felt when he saw me in that meeting.

I step into the library, resolved not to think about Noah Hunter anymore. That lasts all of two minutes as I approach the stack of newly delivered books that need to be shelved and see the title of the one on top: *Romeo and Juliet.* Bleh. I turn it over so I can't see the cover. Noah and I aren't star-crossed lovers. We already had our tragedy and I'm over it, moving on. I grab the stack and start moving along the shelves, placing them exactly where they need to go. Soon enough, I'm so busy with my work that I don't think about Noah at all. Well, not much anyway.

I'm placing the final book on the shelf when the doors open and the beautiful blonde woman I noticed with Gabe earlier walks in, her arm intertwined with one belonging to a stunning brunette with an hourglass figure

I would die for. My body is strong enough. I carry books around all day after all, but I'm still a little soft, and while I have hips and breasts, they aren't as perfectly proportioned as this woman's. I look down at my chest and frown, wishing I had worn my push-up bra today. When I see the two women approaching me, I straighten myself up to my full five and a half feet of height. Meeting new people always makes me anxious and holding myself up high will help me deal with that.

They come to a stop in front of me and the blonde reaches out her hand. "Hi, Caitlin! I'm Amelia Graham and I teach art here at Central. I'm so happy to meet you."

I don't move, too dazzled by her smile for a moment before I remember myself and reach out to grab her hand. "Thanks, Amelia. It's nice to meet you too."

My eyes move over to the brunette and she's studying me with her eyes narrowed. The woman is intimidating to say the least, and not just because she's beautiful. She also looks like she could take someone down a peg or two with just a look and a few choice words. Amelia jabs an elbow into her side and untangles herself from her friend before extending her hand as well. "I'm Madi Graham, and I teach freshmen English."

I blink at the mention of the same name. "Oh, you guys are related?" They are both very pretty, but beyond that they don't really look alike.

Madi laughs and her smile lights up her face. "Yes, but only though marriage. I'm married to Owen. He teaches the AP English classes."

Amelia bumps her shoulder. "We're related by more than marriage. Madi here is my sister from another mister. It's just official now that my brother finally got his head out of his butt and married her."

They smile and interact like lifelong friends and

I'm jealous of their easy comradery. I would love to have a close friend who felt more like family. I have a younger brother, but he's in high school now and we aren't super close. Ironically enough, he's a football player and I think we're just a little too different to have a bond like these two share. Now that I've moved to Sun Valley, I don't have my library friends either. Amelia and Madi seem very friendly, though, and if everyone else at this school is as welcoming, maybe I'll have some new work friends after all.

"Anyways," Amelia says with a little laugh. "We didn't just come over here to introduce ourselves. We wanted to invite you to our girls' night on Friday. We watch movies and eat lots of yummy food. We used to have wine, but now that I'm pregnant, I can't do that and Madi is abstaining in solidarity. Feel free to bring your own alcohol if you like, though." I blink in surprise. They want to hang out with me? I've heard people in small towns were friendly, and I guess it's actually true.

"Yeah, as long as there are Oreos on hand, Ames here can deal with the jealousy of watching someone else drink," Madi says with a smile.

I chuckle. "Oh, I don't really drink, so you won't have any cause to be jealous of me. I do like Oreos, but not all of them. Some of the flavors they keep coming up with are weird to me, like banana split. Who wants to eat a banana split when it's ice cream, let alone a cookie flavor?" I snort and look at Amelia and Madi who are giving me polite smiles. I bite my lip to stop my inane babbling and school my features. *This is why you don't have any friends, Cait. You are just. So. Awkward.*

"Right? Bananas with ice cream sounds totally disgusting to me, and I'm pregnant and will eat just about anything." Amelia chuckles and it eases my worry some. I really need to stop reading into things. "So will you come?"

I think about it and decide I don't have anything to lose by making friends here. Maybe I'll even be able to keep them after I sell Gran's house and move away, if that's what I decide to do. "Sure! It sounds like fun." It also sounds like a social-anxiety-inducing nightmare, but I can suck it up to make some friends.

"Great! My house is under construction at the moment, so we'll meet at Madi's apartment," Amelia says politely.

Madi leans over to the circulation desk and grabs a pen and paper where she jots down her address and both of their phone numbers before handing it to me. "Here you go. You can text if you get lost or anything like that. We'll meet up around six?" She looks at Amelia to confirm the time and when she sees her nod, she turns back to me. "Six o'clock on Friday then."

"Do I need to bring anything?" I've never really had a girls' night before and I want to make a good impression. I can't really cook or bake well, though, so that could be a problem.

"Just yourself. Oh, and we usually hang out in our comfy clothes, so you can change before you head over if you want," Amelia explains.

"I basically live in comfy clothes when I'm not at work, so that should be easy enough," I reply. It's totally true too. The minute I get home I transfer into cutoffs or pajamas.

"My kind of gal," Madi says with a wink. "See you on Friday, Cait." Madi turns to leave but stops abruptly. "Oh, how do you take your coffee?" she asks abruptly.

I look at her, a little puzzled at the question, but I answer anyway. "Oh, um. Vanilla latte with a sprinkle of cinnamon, but I usually don't drink coffee after lunch, so

I won't need any Friday night."

"Okay, great. Thanks." With that, Madi moves back toward the door and Amelia waves before she follows her best friend out of the library. I wave back and smile to myself. I have my first get-together with potential friends and I'm really excited about it. A little nervous too, but mostly excited I think. The new emotions swirling around almost make me forget about everything that has happened with Noah. Almost, but not quite.

****

Friday morning rolls around and I am dragging myself from one moment to the next. I've only had two days with students, but I forgot how much energy teenagers have and there have been a steady stream of them in the library since classes started. I should be happy that so many kids are interested in reading and that the library feels safe for them, but it's been a little draining having to socialize so much. At the public library, I answered questions and helped people find books and do research, but it didn't happen that often and most people kept to themselves. These kids have been asking all sorts of questions about me since the moment they got here. Some of the students, who I am pretty sure are regulars, weren't satisfied with just the basics of name and work history, they wanted to know my marital status, if I want children, and which teachers I think are hot. I told them I wouldn't answer the last question as it was inappropriate, but really I was afraid I'd tell them that the gym coach is the hottest guy on the planet. Luckily, they took my original answer at face value and moved on.

With heavy steps, I walk up to the library and unlock the double doors. Some of the regulars told me they like to gather here in the morning to work on a graphic novel they're trying to get published. I love that they're so creative and I want to be able to provide the safe space for them to produce their work, so I got here a little early to be ready for their arrival. Unfortunately, in my haste, I forgot to drink my coffee and I am paying for it now. I can picture the full mug of light-brown liquid sitting on the tile countertop in my kitchen and I groan. I could really use a hit of caffeine right now.

The lights come on with a flick of the switch and I amble back to my office where I drop my things. It's a little chilly in here, so I wrap my big fuzzy blanket around my shoulders while I get everything set up for the morning. I'm walking around the big, open-concept main library room, turning on computers and shelving books that didn't get put back yesterday afternoon when I hear a door open. When I flick my gaze over to the entrance, my feet freeze in place. Noah is walking in holding a coffee cup and a paper bag. I'm not sure what he's doing here and I don't think I want to know. Seeing him after all this time is still unsettling, even more so since my stupid heart and body are reacting to him like they used to. My heart threatens to beat out of my chest, my limbs feeling all warm and tingly, and I feel my whole body leaning toward his. I'm still upset at what happened, but that doesn't stop me from wanting to curl up on his lap and plant a big ole kiss on his full lips. I wonder what they taste and feel like. I take in his tight sweatpants and formfitting athletic shirt and drool starts pooling in my mouth. He comes up to me and stops short of invading my personal space, but still close enough that I can smell his fresh laundry and pine forest scent. God, he smells good. He used to just smell like Irish Spring soap, but whatever he's using now is an improvement.

"Hey there, Caity-bug. I brought you a coffee."

He holds one of the cups out to me and I wrap my hands around my torso. I feel soft fabric and realize I've still got the fuzzy blanket over my shoulder. Darn it, I probably look like a crazy person all wrapped up like this. I shrug the blanket off and toss it over a chair.

"I told you not to call me that. And I don't drink coffee," I lie, jutting my chin out defiantly. I was just wishing for a cup moments ago, but I won't drink his coffee. I bet it comes with strings attached.

He blushes, looking a little abashed. "Sorry about that, Caitlin. I'll try not to slip up again." He's still holding the coffee out toward me and gives the cup a little wiggle. "You sure you don't want this, though, darlin'? It's a vanilla latte with a sprinkle of cinnamon." He holds up the little bag next to the coffee in his other hand. "I even brought you a chocolate-chip muffin to go with it. I remember you used to sneak bites of those in the library when you thought no one was looking."

My eyes shoot to his at the mention of the memory. He noticed that? I shouldn't be excited about him having observed me doing that, but I am. My heart skips a beat and I can feel the corners of my mouth twitching with the need to smile. I'm softening toward him and I can't have that, so I put my walls back up. "Why are you here, Noah?"

He sighs. "I told you, I'm going to prove I'm not the same stupid kid I was in high school. Give me a chance to do that. Please?" He pleads with puppy dog eyes and I cave just a little. My walls might as well be made of cardboard.

"Fine. I'll take the coffee and the muffin, but only because I'm tired and hungry. Not for any other reason." I grab the coffee and bag out of his hands before taking a sip from the cup. The coffee is warm and sweet with just a hint of spice at the end. I'm not sure where he got the coffee, but I need to find out because it is perfection. I moan as the flavors coat my tongue and lick the few drops that remain from my lips. I look over at Noah and he has a slightly pained look on his face. I may not want to be concerned about him, but I can't help that I am. "Are you okay?"

He swallows thickly. "Yea," he squeaks out before clearing his throat. "Yes, yes, I'm fine. So, you like the coffee?" He takes a deep breath and releases it. Maybe he's nervous too, so I cut him a little more slack.

"Yes, it's delicious. Where did you get it?" I ask, taking another drag of the necessary caffeine.

He clucks his tongue and shakes his head at me. "I think I'll keep this one to myself, darlin'. I need all the excuses I can get to see you, and I'm not giving up the opportunity to win you over with good coffee," he admits with a smile.

I open my mouth and close it. Win me over? He was serious? "You're really going to come bring me coffee every morning?" I eye him skeptically. I don't believe it and I won't until I see it.

He narrows his gaze at me. "I can tell I still have a long way to go before you'll believe I'm for real. That's okay, though. I'm willing to put in the effort." The front door of the library opens and the graphic novel kids come in. They wave at me and smile and shout hey to Noah. It seems he's still the popular kid, even as a teacher. He looks at them before turning back to me. "I'm going to go, but I want you to know it's only because I don't want to share your attention. You have a nice day now, darlin'." He looks over at the group of students one more time and sees that they're busy unpacking their bags and chatting to one another. He turns back and leans down, quickly kissing my cheek before heading out the door.

My eyes are wide and I bring my hand up to touch

the spot on my face where his lips were. It's warm to the touch and I'm sure that's from the blush that's happening all over my face. The corners of my mouth lift into a small smile and I don't bother to try and stop it this time. I don't know if this is real or some kind of game to him, but I really want to believe Noah's intentions are honorable. I just hope I can keep my heart locked up tight enough so there's no way he can break it again.

Chapter Eight
Noah

The sound of sneakers squeaking along the gymnasium floor is starting to grate on my nerves, but it's my own fault. I'm the one that decided wind sprints would be part of the beginning-of-the-year fitness assessment. My timer stops and I blow the whistle to signal the end of the trial and I watch as twenty-five boys all but collapse onto the bleachers, huffing and puffing as they try to catch their breath.

"All right, boys. How'd you do?" I call out to the assembly of teens and I get nothing but groans in reply. I chuckle. "That good, huh? Well, I hope you enjoyed yourselves because up next we have a series of jump squats followed by pull-ups and we'll round out the period with a nice little jog around the gym to cool ourselves off. What do you think?" I'm met with more groans and blow my whistle. "Go get some water and meet me back here in five."

The boys scramble to the water fountain and proceed to push each other in and out of line in an effort to be the first to refuel. I laugh to myself as I mark some things down on my clipboard with my pen. God, I love this job. I could spend all day teaching these kids. They are endlessly entertaining and because I'm a gym coach, I don't have to deal with too many discipline issues or kids stressing out over tests and assignments. I do still have to include those things, but most teens don't stress over having to write an essay on the merits of physical fitness or their favorite athlete.

This is my third period and it is full of freshmen, so I need to be sure to leave an extra five minutes for shower time. They're not used to the schedule yet and if they don't get enough time to clean off, they end up hosing themselves with enough body spray to choke an ox. They scamper back over to where I'm standing and I spend the rest of the period demonstrating some jump squats and pull-ups for them before we all jog around the gym. I like to do the exercises with them most of the time. It's light work compared to what I normally do, so I don't even really work up a sweat, and it's always easier to get the students to do things when they see I'm willing to do them too. Plus, it keeps me in decent shape.

While the freshmen shower, I set up some equipment in the weight room for my lifting class. It's mostly comprised of members of the football team, but every now and then you'll get others, and I was pleased to see a good number of girls in class this year. It's nice to have a mix and it keeps the boys' behavior in line. It's also hilarious to watch some of these guys try to impress the girls with their lifting prowess, though I do have to remind the more overzealous individuals not to overdo it to win a date. I make my way back to the locker room in time for the bell to ring and the freshmen to scurry out. "See you boys tomorrow!" I call out as they run off to their next class.

I watch a few members of my next class file into the locker room, doling out high fives and fist bumps to most before I head over to the weight room to meet everyone. Once everyone is changed and in the room, I walk around and hand out the personalized lifting plans we came up with during the first few days of school. "All right everyone, listen up! We will be spending the next forty-five minutes working through your plans. You already know the rules for wiping down your machine and swapping during sets if your machine is occupied. I will be moving around the room to answer questions, demonstrate exercises, and provide spot support should you need it. Any questions?"

"No, coach!" the students shout in unison.

This class is easily my favorite as everyone already knows me and knows the drill. They come in here to get some work done and don't get too distracted while they do it. There is the occasional horsing around and peacocking, but for the most part, its smooth sailing. I blow my whistle and watch them get to work. I walk around the room and see that, for the most part, everyone is doing well and they don't need much direction from me. I spy one of my linebackers attempting a dead lift and if he keeps going, he'll throw his back out.

I stride over and drop my clipboard on the ground. "O'Sullivan. Keep that back flat or you're going to hurt yourself."

He does as I instruct and puffs out a, "Sorry, coach."

"No worries. I would hate to lose a linebacker before the big game next week." I would hate for the kid to miss out on the game too. He's talented and could go pro if we're lucky enough to ever get a scout in the stands.

The rest of the class period goes by quickly and once the bell rings, I make my way over to the office and check my phone. I have a text from Owen asking about game night and I reply with a, "Hell, yes!" There's no game for me to coach tonight and I could use a little video game therapy. Maybe my boys will have some ideas that could help me win over my Caity-bug. I think she's warming up to me and I plan to bring her coffee and a muffin every day, just like I told her, but I need to get a little more creative. Both Gabe and Owen had issues with their girls and came out on top in the end, so maybe they can help me.

****

I knock on the teal door to Gabe and Amelia's house. It's a nice little fixer-upper that the two bought and moved into shortly after learning they were having a baby. I've been here a few times already to help Gabe with some of the home improvement projects he's wanted to get done before the baby arrives, and each time I do the place looks more and more like a home for the little family. We've already redone the wood floors and painted every room in the place. He wanted my help to rewire the house, but I told him that's where I draw the line. There's no way I'm risking electrocution so Gabe can save money on hiring a licensed electrician. He agreed that burning down his new house probably wasn't wise and got a contractor.

The door swings open and Amelia is there to greet me. "Noah! Hi, come on in." I step inside and give her a hug, making sure to give enough room for her growing baby belly. Her honey-blonde hair is up in a high ponytail and she's wearing some stretchy pants and a large t-shirt. She's normally a little more dressed up, but I know better than to say anything. She must see the confusion written on my face because she frowns and points at my face. "Not one word about my clothes, Mister. It's girls' night and that means I get my comfy clothes." She get a little teary-eyed and sniffles. "Besides, it's not my fault none of my old clothes fit." She sniffles again and I panic. I have never had to deal with a weepy pregnant woman before and I have no clue what to do.

Luckily, Gabe comes from around the corner and pulls her into a side hug before kissing her temple. "You are beautiful, *querida*. You are growing our baby and would look amazing no matter what you were wearing.

Our little one is so lucky to have you as their mama," he coos at his fiancée in soft, soothing tones.

Amelia smiles up at him and her eyes clear instantly. Gabe steers her toward the living room and glares at me over his shoulder. *Sorry,* I mouth at him. I'll need to practice schooling my features so I can avoid this in the future.

I take the six-pack of beer I brought over to the kitchen and place it in the fridge. I can smell something wonderful coming from the oven and I am sure it's one of Amelia's delicious casseroles or baked goods. One nice thing about all my friends shacking up is that the quality of food at our game nights has improved exponentially. I hear the doorbell ring and glance over to the entryway to see Owen coming in. I nod at him and watch as Amelia takes off right after she hugs her brother.

Owen walks into the kitchen and claps my shoulder. "Hey, man. What's up?"

"Not much. Just getting myself psyched up for some serious gaming. It's been too long." When Owen and I first met, our game nights were a weekly event. As time passed and we got busier, they became bimonthly and then monthly. I'm hoping that the two of them moving in with their significant others doesn't mean we'll hang out even less.

"Yea, it has. Get ready to have your ass kicked in Mario Kart!" he brags loudly.

"Please, you're going down hard, Graham," I tell him, more than confident in my own video gaming skills.

We continue to chirp at each other for a minute before Gabe walks into the room and punches my arm. "Ow, man. What was that for?"

"You really have to ask? What did you say to her?" He's clearly irritated, but I have a feeling it has more to do with the roller coaster of emotions his fiancée is riding on than with anything I may have done.

"I said nothing. I merely looked at her clothes and she interpreted my facial expressions negatively," I admit. It's not my fault she's pregnant and her hormones are all over the place.

Gabe sighs. "Ugh, okay. Next time just bring a box of Oreos and don't look directly at her. Just kind of play dead, like if you saw a grizzly," he says with a totally straight face.

Owen barks a laugh. "Did you just liken my sister to a bear?" he asks, both amused and irritated on his sister's behalf.

"I'm not sure what you think you heard, Owen." Gabe strolls over to the oven and pulls out a platter covered in tamales and another pan filled with cheesecake brownies. "But if you want to get fed this evening, I highly suggest you think long and hard about forgetting anything I just said," he says deadpan.

I crack a smile just as Owen frowns. "That's not cool, man. You know how much I love food," Owen gripes. The man is an eating machine, so threatening his food chain is a surefire way to get him to cave.

Gabe just smiles serenely in return. "I do. So what did you hear earlier?"

"Nothing," Owen mumbles sadly.

Gabe nods and grabs some plates from the cabinets. We dish up our food, grab some beers, and make our way to the family room where the Nintendo has been set up. I place my beer bottle on the coffee table when I feel a wooden coaster hit my chest. I look over at Gabe who is staring at me with a raised brow. "Really, man?"

"When we're at your place, we'll live by your rules, but when you're at my house, we'll live by..." he trails of.

"Amelia's," I cut in, knowing full well she's the one who wears the pants in the family.

He narrows his eyes at me before replying. "Yes, Amelia's," he admits, but he doesn't look the least bit put out by it.

I smile and Owen chuckles but tries to turn it into a cough when Gabe's head whips around to him. "And whose rules are you living by, Owen?"

"Touché," he mutters, knowing very well that he would totally do whatever his wife asked him to do.

My grin widens until both turn to me. "Yuck it up while you can, friend," Owen tells me. "The minute you get your girl and start getting led around by the you know what, I'll be there with a big, fat 'I told you so'."

"Well, you better have it ready soon because I plan on winning my girl over ASAP," I say smugly, puffing out my chest in a victory I haven't earned.

Gabe raises his brow. "Really? The look of horror on her face when she spotted you in that meeting the other day says otherwise," he says with a chuckle.

I give him a withering look. "She was not horrified, just surprised. We talked and I brought her some coffee this morning. I think she's coming around. I *hope* she's coming around." If she doesn't come around eventually, I'm not sure what I'll do.

"Well, sometimes you must be patient. Not everyone is ready to jump into a relationship," Gabe says before taking a large bite of tamale. I remember he and Amelia had a rocky start, but they're engaged now, so maybe there's hope for me yet.

"Yeah, you might need to slow down on this one, man." Owen takes a swig of beer and wipes his mouth on the back of his hand. "If what you told us the other day is your version of events, I'm guessing hers is more than a little bit worse. It might take her a while to get over it."

"I get that, really I do, but I've been wishing for a do-over for so long and I'm ready to go all out to prove my worth." I mean every word I just said. I will do whatever it takes to get my second chance.

"And how do you plan on doing that?" Owen asks.

"I have a couple of ideas, but I was hoping you guys would help me. You know, since I played cupid for you two not so long ago." I didn't really do much for either of them, just gave them a little push or nudge when they needed it, but I'm not above using the guilt card to get some help.

"Noah, we're friends. You don't need to bargain for our help," Gabe tells me, dusting brownie crumbs off his hands.

"Yea, you need to beg for our help," Owen says over his shoulder as he makes his way to the kitchen to grab more food.

"Dick," I mutter.

"I heard that," he singsongs from the kitchen.

"Anyway," Gabe says rolling his eyes at our childish antics, clearly the most mature out of the three of us. "You've got a fine line to walk. You kind of want to remind her of the good times you had together without going so far that it brings up the bad stuff too."

"How do I do that?" I plead.

"I don't know, man. She's your girl, you're going to have to feel it out. It's been a long time since you two were friends. You've changed, so she probably has too."

"Yea," Owen says reentering the room. "Get to know the person she is now. Build a relationship and the past won't be as much of a factor."

"Thanks, guys. Let's hope you're right. Caitlin has always been all sweetness and light. Here's hoping she gives me another chance." I raise my beer bottle and the two men clink theirs with mine. We move on to other topics as we continue to eat and play throughout the evening, but as I'm diving back to my place, my mind wanders again to Caity. I hope she'll let me get to know her and trust that I would never break her heart the way I did back then. I'm a better man now, and I'm going to prove it.

Chapter Nine
Caitlin

The parking lot of the apartment complex is almost full, so it takes me a few minutes to find a spot for my little blue hybrid vehicle. Once I park, I take one last look at my outfit. They said comfy clothes, and I took that to heart. I'm wearing black lounge pants and a blue tank top with the Captain America shield on it. My hair was a little wild after the day, but I managed to wrangle it into a braid. I think I look cute, actually. Feeling confident, I grab my purse and head outside.

I find Madi's apartment easily enough and knock on the door. Madi greets me wearing flannel pajama pants and a pink tank. Amelia stands behind her wearing yoga pants and a t-shirt and I release a breath, knowing that I dressed appropriately. "Come in, come in," Madi says, waving her hand as she moves to the side to let me in the apartment. The rooms are decorated in an eclectic mix of masculine and feminine styles, lots of black and beige with random splashes of color coming from the bookshelf and throw pillows. I take it all in and Madi chuckles. "It's a style all its own, I know, but until we find a house, it's the best I could do," she says with a smile.

I chuckle. "That's okay. I'm living in my gran's old place and the kitchen hasn't been redone since the 1980s, so anything other than celery-green linoleum is the height of design if you ask me," I tell her. Madi smiles and walks toward the small kitchen that's covered in white cabinets and a tile backsplash. As I follow her, an enticing aroma wafts over me. I drop my purse on the counter with a thunk, inhaling the meaty, cheesy scent.

"What smells so amazing?"

"Oh, that would be one of Madi's awesome casseroles. She somehow manages to make one-pan meals taste delicious," Amelia explains, beaming with pride at her friend's cooking ability.

"Aww, thanks, bestie." Madi gives Amelia a side hug and I'm once again in awe of how easily these two socialize with one another. "I made bacon cheeseburger casserole tonight. It's kind of like an American version of Shepard's pie," she explains to me.

"Well, it smells delicious and I can't wait to try it." I mean it too. I don't normally eat a lot of cheeseburgers, but it smells too good to pass up and anything other than takeout will be a treat for me.

"Excellent. It will be ready in a minute." Madi glances down at my tank top and chuckles as she elbows Amelia. "It's so funny that you're wearing that shirt," she says, her eyes filled with amusement.

I look down at my top and feel my brow furrow. It looks normal to me and I glance back up at Madi, confused. "Why is it funny?"

Amelia laughs along with her friend. "Well, because we know a certain someone who wears a Captain America costume just about every Halloween." Her expression is kind, not a trace of taunting, but I feel like I'm the butt of some inside joke.

"Okaaay," I say, still not understanding what the heck is going on.

"And we'll be eating his favorite casserole too," Madi says as she pulls the food from the oven. The smell is stronger now and my mouth waters, but I'm still not really getting the joke.

"I don't get it," I admit. My chest tightens. I have a bad feeling and I hope this isn't some type of mean girls situation. They both seemed so nice, but of course I've been fooled before. My gut twists at the thought that I've stumbled into another opportunity for someone to mock me, and my fingers twist anxiously.

Amelia must see the wariness on my face because she comes over and touches my arm. "Hey," she speaks softly. "We're not laughing at you or anything like that, I promise. It's just funny that you wore that tank because the one who always wears that costume is Noah."

"Oh," I breathe out. I'm glad they aren't making fun of me, but I didn't think I'd be having to deal with all that drama tonight and I don't like feeling blindsided. "You guys are friends with Noah? Is that why you invited me?"

Amelia bites her lip and the gesture is so familiar to me, I automatically soften toward her and try to not seem so defensive. "Well, yes, we are friends with Noah, but we didn't invite you here because of that." Madi looks at her and she sighs. "Well, that's not the only reason. He told us what happened between you guys back in the day and we thought you could use some friends. It was obvious that seeing him rattled you a bit."

Madi snorts as she scoops some of the casserole onto three plates. "Understatement."

"I'll admit, it was a bit of a shock." It's nice that they are offering to be supportive friends to me, but it's a little confusing because they're also friends with Noah. Maybe that's a good thing. He told me he's changed and they would be able to tell me whether that's true. I tug at the hem of my tank, suddenly more nervous than before. "He talked to me after the meeting and apologized, though. And he brought me coffee, so I think he's trying to smooth things over."

Amelia nods and Madi comes over to hand us our plates. "If we're going to dish, I need to get comfortable." She nods over to the living room and I trail behind them before kicking off my sandals and taking a seat on a very comfy-looking blue chair.

I take a bite of the casserole and groan appreciatively. "This is so good," I tell Madi around a mouthful of food. The bacon, beef, and cheese pair surprisingly well with the mashed potato topping. I can taste tomato sauce and mustard and the whole thing is like a burger and fries at the same time. "I definitely need the recipe for this." It probably won't taste as good as it does now with me behind the stove, but it's so yummy, I'd be willing to give it a try.

Amelia chuckles. "It's Noah's favorite too." I don't like the feeling of jealousy that courses through me. Madi is happily married, so it shouldn't matter if she cooks for Noah or not. It shouldn't matter anyway because I shouldn't care who is cooking for Noah. Argh! *Get it together, Cait.*

Madi gives me a knowing look. "Noah only eats it when I make it for their game nights, so there's no need to be jealous," she says with a smirk.

"I'm not jealous." I pout. I was totally jealous.

Amelia snorts. "It's okay to still feel things for him, you know." She moves next to me and pats my knee. "What happened to you guys in high school was awful, but he's a really good guy, Caitlin."

He does seem like a good guy, but what happened was awful and it's resurfacing now. I feel my eyes well up with tears. I don't want to feel the pain again, but it's coming back anyway. "I do still feel things." I sniffle, shaking my head quickly. "But I don't want to. I'm so confused. I was so hurt and it stuck with me for a long time. I thought I moved past all that, but it's still right here." I tap my chest and feel a tear fall down my face.

"Oh, sweetie." Amelia gets up and hugs me and it's like a dam bursts. Everything I felt back then comes rushing to the surface, and I let it all out through the tears that pour down my face. Amelia rubs my back in soothing circles. I go on like this for a couple of minutes before I lean back and Madi hands me a tissue. "I didn't mean to make you cry," Amelia says regretfully, her own eyes looking a little misty.

I blow my nose and swipe away the moisture on my cheeks. "It's okay. I think that has been building since I saw him on Monday." I take a deep breath and let it out slowly. I'm a little embarrassed at my display of emotion and wipe my nose a little more. This is probably why I don't have friends. "Sorry if I'm ruining your girls' night," I mutter sadly.

Madi chuckles. "If crying ruined girls' night, then Ames and I have ruined our fair share, believe me." She hands me a fresh tissue and I use it to wipe off my face. "Besides, it's good to get all this stuff out so you can work through it. You need to process the pain before you can move on."

I nod. "That sounds really smart."

"Well, I do go to therapy, so I have all kinds of useful tidbits." She smiles and scoops some casserole into her mouth, chewing thoughtfully before she continues. "I had some stuff to work through with Owen, and Ames and Gabe had their own issues as well, so it's not like you and Noah are the only couple who have troubles."

"We're not a couple, though," I protest. Do I want to be a couple? *Yes,* I think before I scold myself for being so weak.

"Not yet," Amelia mumbles before shoving a bite of food into her mouth.

Madi shoots her a look. "True, but if you set aside all the pain from that day, how do you feel about him?"

I take a moment to think about it before shaking my head. When it comes to Noah, my mind is a jumbled mess of sadness, pain, nostalgia, and a good amount of lust. I don't look deeper than that, worried that I'll feel another "L" word still floating around in there. "I don't know. Everything I ever felt or still feel about him is all tangled up in what happened. I just don't know if I can trust my feelings where he's concerned."

"But you do have feelings?" Amelia asks.

"I'll always have feelings for Noah. He was the first man I ever loved." I swallow the lump of emotion that has formed in my throat. "He's the only man I've ever loved," I whisper.

They both smile sadly at me and Madi comes over to wrap me up in a big hug. Her embrace is warm and soft, like the best blanket ever and I instantly feel very comforted. If this is what having friends is like, I really should have put in more of a concerted effort to making some sooner. "I think we've probably drained you of enough emotion for one evening. A bit of a trial by fire tonight, huh?" She laughs and I join her. "How about instead of digging into this anymore tonight, we watch a movie?"

"Can I just say one last thing?" Amelia asks and I nod my agreement. "Try to keep an open mind where Noah is concerned. We've known him a while, and even though he hasn't really hurt for female attention, I've never seen him look at anyone the way he looks at you."

"How's that?" I venture, slightly worried yet hopeful of the answer.

She smiles. "Like you're different. Special. He may play himself off as a bit of a goofy jock, but he feels things deeply, and I can tell he has some deep feelings for you."

I take another breath, not quite ready to deal with all the emotions bubbling up after that revelation. I am ready to express my gratitude to these two awesome women, however. "Thanks, you guys."

Madi claps her hands. "Okay, now we have an important decision to make. Do we watch *Magic Mike* or *Magic Mike XXL*?"

I giggle. "I haven't seen either, so whichever is good for you."

Amelia gasps. "You haven't seen either?" She turns to Madi. "Looks like it's a double-feature night," she says, doing a little dance in her spot.

Madi squeals and hops up to grab the remote. "Four hours of hot guys dancing? Yes, please!"

I laugh at these two sweet, caring, funny women and despite the emotional breakdown I had, I feel better having shared it all. I'm so glad I came tonight. I wish I had shared the burden of this with someone earlier on. Maybe then I would have already moved passed it. There are some more things I need to work through and think about, but I'm going to try to do what Amelia asked of me and keep an open mind about Noah. I'm not sure I can say the same thing about my heart, though. At least, not just yet. For now, I'm still going to keep it locked up tight.

Chapter Ten
Noah

The barbell clangs as I drop it back on to the rack and sit up on the weight bench. I'm covered in sweat and I can feel the burn in my muscles from pushing myself a little harder this morning. I couldn't help it. Ever since Caity came back in my life, I have had energy to burn and have been using the gym as my go-to spot to rid myself of the excess. My body has been buzzing with awareness for over a week and I can't seem to sit still. I head over to the stretch area, plop down on the ground, and spread my legs out in front of me. I reach for my toes and enjoy the feel of the muscles loosening. I glance down at my sports watch and see that it's already 6:15. I'd better get a move on if I'm going to be on time for school. Luckily for me, the first period of the day is my prep time, so even if I'm in a rush I won't have to walk straight into the classroom.

I hop up off the mat and smile at the two other early birds here at the gym as I walk toward the exit. I head outside and lightly jog over to my apartment that sits on the bottom floor right next to the leasing office. It's prime real estate for a guy like me who enjoys the free coffee and cookies they put out daily. Can I afford my own coffee and cookies? Of course I can, but I'm not going to pass up freebies when it saves me time and money. With all the free food I enjoy here and at The Goat, you'd never know I was actually a pretty decent cook. That's probably one of the few useful things my dad taught me. Of course, most of that was because he wanted to micromanage my diet while I was playing football in order to "get the most out of my performance," but it worked and now I can grill up a steak and veggies with the best of 'em.

I walk inside my apartment and take a quick look around. Despite having lived here for four years, the walls are empty and the living room contains nothing but an old leather couch and a television. I catch a glimpse of my guitar in the corner and tell myself I'll practice a little later if I have time. It's a hobby I picked up after football wasn't an option anymore. I'm not going to be the next greatest country star, but I can play a few of my favorite tunes and get by with most others. I make my way into the bedroom that has a bed and a dresser and I wonder why I haven't done more to make this a home. I guess when you move around as much as I did, you learn not to decorate. Why bother putting up posters or paintings I'll just have to take down in a few months? Things are a little different now, so maybe I'll change that, but I don't think this is the place I want to make a home. Caity's green eyes pop into my head and I know why I haven't bothered to put more of a mark on this apartment. I haven't made a home here because before I didn't have someone to make it with. That's going to change soon, though. Hopefully.

I step into the shower and enjoy the feel of the warm water loosening my sore muscles. I wish I could take longer to fully appreciate it, but instead I soap up and wash my hair as quickly as possible. Once I'm out and dried off, I walk over to my dresser and proceed to put on my work clothes: basketball shorts, a Central High School t-shirt, and a hoodie in case the gym is cold. One more reason I love my job is the fact that I get to wear this day in and day out. I run over to the fridge and grab a pre-made breakfast sandwich and a protein shake before I head out the door.

Once I'm at my truck, I hop inside and drink the

shake as I pull out of the parking lot. I turn the radio on to the local country station and briefly lament the fact that they don't play the country music I grew up with. Don't get me wrong, some of the songs are great, just not as good as George Strait and Garth Brooks. Still, I sing along with Keith Urban because I can't not sing along to a catchy tune as I move on from my shake to my breakfast sandwich. I'm just wiping the last of the crumbs out of my stubble as I pull into the drive-thru for Jolt Coffee Shop. After ordering Caity's drink and my own black coffee, I get back on the road and pull into the lot of the school ten minutes later. I'm arriving at the same time as a lot of the students, so I'm not very late.

I grab my bag from the passenger seat and after slinging it over my shoulder, I grab the two coffee cups and lock up the truck. With eager steps, I walk through the gate and head over to the library, weaving through the kids as they scurry off to class. A kid exits the library and I snag the door with my elbow before it closes completely, forcing it open wider and making my way through and toward the circulation desk where I already see Caity working away at the computer. Her long, red curls are draped over one shoulder. She's wearing a green sweater over a light-gray dress and her face scrunches up adorably as she concentrates on the screen in front of her. What would it feel like to have all that concentration pointed at me? Pretty damn good I imagine, and it steels my resolve to make her mine.

"Your coffee, ma'am." I place the travel mug down in front of her and she blinks up at me and smiles. It takes my breath away and I have to make a concentrated effort to not fall at her feet and beg her to give me shot. "Um, I got you a travel mug. I figured if I was going to be bringing you coffee every day, I should cut back on the waste."

She looks at the mug and laughs. It's a melodious sound I haven't heard in ages, but it's just as beautiful as I remember and I swear a silent vow to make it happen more often. Seeing her happy is a gift I want to receive as often as possible and knowing I'm the cause of it makes it even better. "This is great, thanks, Noah." She picks up the mug that says, *Instant Librarian, Just Add Coffee*, and takes a small sip. She licks her lips and I bite back a groan. She did that last week and I nearly embarrassed myself with my arousal. It's been a while and she is very tempting. The hot librarian look was never one I went for until she was the one performing the job, now it's all I fantasize about. On more than one occasion I have pictured her dragging me into the stacks and slamming me against the shelves before kissing me senseless. Coughing, I try to clear the image from my mind and calm my libido. "So, this makes five days in a row for coffee delivery. You really meant what you said?" she asks, blinking her big doe-eyes up at me.

I get lost in her gaze for a moment before nodding. "Yes, ma'am. I am a man of my word and I told you I would bring you coffee every day and I plan to do just that—and more—if you'll let me." Her cheeks blush and I love that her mind probably went somewhere a little dirty Just as mine did. "Oh, nothing like that yet, sweet cheeks. I need to earn your trust first." Her face is beet-red now and I chuckle. "I was thinking maybe you'd let me take you out to dinner this weekend."

She shakes her head and smiles. "Uh, that's what I was thinking anyway." *Liar.* "But, um, I can't do dinner. I have a lot do around the house. I'm trying to fix it up, but I don't have a lot of home renovation skills, so it's slow going," she says, shrugging one of her slender shoulders.

Hmm. I don't like the sound of her using this

potentially lengthy home project as an excuse to not go out. She could be telling me no all year long. "Well, I just so happen to have some experience in home improvement. So, you give me your address and I'll come by Saturday morning with breakfast and my toolbox. Does that work for you, darlin'?" She bites her lip as she thinks over my proposal. I remember her doing that all the time in high school and I like it as much now as I did back then. Seeing her hurt herself, even in such a small way, tears me up inside. Caity should only ever feel good things, never bad. I reach over and pull her lip free with my thumb. "Treat those lips nicely, please." I run my forefinger under her chin and she trembles. She may be hesitant to let me into her heart again, but at the very least she's attracted to me and that is something I can work with.

She pushes her chair back slightly and my hand falls away. "I don't know if I like that idea, Noah," she tells me, her expression wary.

"What's not to like?" I ask, smiling to try and put her at ease. "You get some free labor from a qualified party and I'll be making you breakfast to boot."

She starts to bite her lip again before I school her with a look and she rubs them together instead. She closes her eyes and takes a deep breath. The word "okay" quietly makes its way out of her mouth on an exhale.

"Great!" I shout before she can change her mind. Finding a slip of paper and a tiny pencil, I smile as I hand them over to her. "Give me your address and I'll be over around eight. I have to coach on Friday night, so that's as early as I can commit to." She writes down her address and hands me the paper. When I go to grab it, I brush my fingers against hers and look into her eyes. "Thanks, Caitlin. I'll be by tomorrow with another coffee for you." I turn to leave when I hear her call out over my shoulder.

"Caity!" she tells me. I turn around and face her, hope blooming in my chest. "You can call me Caity."

A small smile comes across her gorgeous face and my heart nearly bursts out from behind my rib cage. I smile brightly at her declaration. It's not her old nickname, but it's a start. "Thank you, Caity." I tip my imaginary hat and catch another glimpse of her smile before I head to the exit.

Once I'm outside I take a deep inhale of the fresh, late summer air. It's warm and I can feel the heat all over my body, but I know it has nothing to do with the temperature and everything to do with the sweet little librarian I just left. I've enjoyed our little visits, but I'm looking forward to some real quality time together. Saturday morning cannot come soon enough.

Chapter Eleven
Caitlin

The sunlight streams through the window and hits me square in the face, barely causing me to stir since I slept like the dead last night. Noah is coming over this morning, and even though he knows this house is a work in progress, I still wanted to clean up as much as I could and spent half the night putting laundry away, moving paint cans, shoving boxes into the garage, and scrubbing the bathroom until it sparkled. I also cleaned the kitchen since he said he was making me breakfast, being sure to take out the trash that was piled high with my takeout boxes. Groggily, I smile at the thought of Noah Hunter in my kitchen and try to tamp down the excitement I feel as well. I don't want to get my hopes up too high. He's determined, I will give him that, but he always was, so I shouldn't be surprised that hasn't changed. But what else hasn't changed? Will he still break my heart? I'm starting to think that's less of a possibility, but I need to know for sure.

Rubbing my eyes, my hand slaps aimlessly at the top of my nightstand before grabbing my glasses. They are the same basic frames I have favored since high school and since I take my contacts out at night, I won't be able to see a thing without them. The loud chiming of the doorbell causes my head to whip over to the clock on my nightstand. It's 7:55 in the morning and I belatedly realize I never set my alarm last night. Crap on a cracker. I nearly jump out of my skin when it rings a second time, quickly hopping out of bed and heading down the hall toward the front door. "Coming!" I call out just before I swing the door wide open. Standing outside in all his male perfection is Noah, wearing jeans that are slung low on his hips, clinging to his muscular thighs in a way that should be illegal, and a tight navy t-shirt that shows off his manly chest. His messy brown hair is covered with a ball cap and he has a bag in his arms. When my gaze finally lands on his face, I see that his expression is pleased as his eyes widen slightly.

"Well, good morning to me," he says, his tone low and filled with gratification. His hazel eyes rake up and down my body, and I feel goose bumps break out across my skin in its wake despite the fact that the look he gave me was filled with pure heat. Ducking my head to hide the blush on my face, I look down at myself and see that I'm wearing nothing but a baggy black t-shirt, my boy-short underwear with the Batman symbol on the rear, and knee-length black Batman socks. "If that's what you show up in when they shine the Bat signal, I'm going to be committing a lot more crime."

All his attention causes my nipples to harden into points and I grab the front of my shirt, pulling it away from my body before he can see. "Um, come on in," I manage to sputter out before stepping aside so he can get through. His hard body brushes against mine and it doesn't help my situation any, his nearness causing an ache to form between my legs. I'm going to need a new pair of panties in addition to some new clothes. "I'll just go change," I choke out before spinning around and heading toward the hall.

"No need to change on my account, darlin'. I like that look on you," he says. I don't turn around to see it, but I can hear the smile in his voice.

"Kitchen's on the right," I call over my shoulder before running into my bedroom and slamming the door.

All it took was one heated look from Noah to turn me on brighter than a thousand-watt light bulb and he's only been here for two seconds. This is going to be a long day. Wiping a hand down my face, I move over to the old dresser in the corner and pull out some clothes that I don't mind getting dirty, quickly putting on a bra, some cutoff jean shorts, and a green tank top. I go to the bathroom and brush my teeth before pulling my hair up into a big, sloppy bun. No use trying to do anything more with the case of bed head I was sporting moments ago since Noah's already seen it. Once I'm as ready as I'll ever be, I leave the bedroom and shuffle down the hall to the kitchen, heading inside but halting my steps almost immediately. Noah is standing at my stove, moving eggs around a pan, and humming softly to the country music that is playing low on the radio, He looks so comfortable and is acting like he's lived here his whole life, but I don't find it aggravating, only endearing. With a soft smile at the big man, I lean against the doorframe and take a moment to appreciate the view. Noah's jeans are a little rumpled, but they still are hugging his high, tight rear in the exact right way. His t-shirt is wrinkled, but again, it forms to his bulging muscles. I'm salivating and I know it has nothing to do with the delicious smells coming from the food. "I think I like you starin' at me like that, Caity."

I jump a little in surprise, but then huff a breath when I process what he just said. "I wasn't staring," I grumble. *I was totally staring.* How could I not in the face of such masculine beauty? Still slightly perturbed at being caught, I scoot closer to the stovetop until I'm right next to him and bump him with my shoulder.

He slowly moves his gaze from the pan over to me and an easy smile slowly comes over his face. "You were starin', but that's okay. Like I said, I like it and besides, I was staring at you plenty earlier, so it's only fair," he admits, that easy smile turning into more of a knowing smirk.

"Maybe I don't like you staring at me." I cross my arms over my chest and when he looks down I realize I'm just pushing my boobs up at him, so I drop my arms to my side again.

He chuckles. "Well, if that is really the case, I will stop. I don't want to give you any attention that isn't sincerely wanted." His face grows serious. "Do you really not want me starin' at you, darlin'?"

I nearly swoon at hearing him call me "darlin'" with that delicious Texas accent and tug at the hem of my shirt as I ponder his question. "I shouldn't want you to stare at me," I say stubbornly.

The corner of his mouth twitches. "That didn't answer my question."

I toss my hands up in the air. "Fine! I want you staring at me. I like that you stare at me." I poke him in the chest. "But that doesn't mean I have to be happy about it."

He grabs my finger and brings it up to his mouth and kisses the tip. "As long as I can still stare at you, I'm happy." His tenderness has me melting a little where I stand and the ice around my heart cracks. It's been doing that a lot in the last week and I know it's only going to happen more often the longer I'm around Noah. God, why does he have to be so darn sweet to me? It's hard to resist, but I need to be strong.

"Well, as long as you're happy," I say quietly.

He turns off the stove and puts down the spatula before stepping closer to me and placing his hands on my hips. I look down at where they grip me, liking the sight of his golden skin on my body, and then back up to his eyes. He has a serious look on his face, but it clears up and that easy smile is back. He starts pushing me backward and doesn't stop until my legs hit a chair at the kitchen table and I'm forced to sit down. "Nuh-uh, darlin'. I want you to be happy too, so why don't you just grab a seat and I'll feed you before you get too hangry?"

"I don't get hangry," I say indignantly.

He backs away from me with both hands raised. "That's something a hangry person would say." He moves around the kitchen and I watch as Noah plates up some eggs, bacon, and buttered toast, and it's hard not to just sit and admire how good he looks. He's attractive and has an amazing body, anyone can see that, but he also just looks so good in my little kitchen, nonchalantly putting together food for us with a little smile on his face. He's still so laid-back, but I also know how responsible he is with his teaching and coaching duties. He really does seem like the same person, only older and hopefully wiser.

My reverie is disrupted when Noah places a plate and a glass of water in front of me before taking a seat across the table and digging into his own meal. I cast my gaze at him and stare for a minute, not moving my eyes away until I see him move his fork over to tap the edge of my plate. "Eat," he grumbles at me around a mouthful of bacon. A smile pulls at the corner of my lips and I comply, raising a bite of the scrambled eggs to my mouth and moaning when the soft texture and savory flavor hit my tongue. I didn't know I liked eggs this much until I wasn't the one who was cooking them. Eagerly, I grab a piece of bacon and sink my teeth into the crisp, fatty strip of pork before moaning again. I have always loved bacon, but it tastes even better this morning. I wiggle in my seat as I chew, excited for the first meal I didn't make myself or grab from a takeout place in God knows how long, when I hear a fork drop. I look up and see Noah sit back in his chair and drag a hand down his face before looking at me with fire in his eyes. "Hell, Caity. I'm glad you enjoy my cooking, but I need you to stop making those noises, okay?"

I swallow the food in my mouth and flush, embarrassed. "Sorry." I pick up a napkin, wiping my mouth and trying to cover up my face a bit. "I didn't realize I was such a noisy eater. I'll try and keep it down."

I reach over to grab my water glass when Noah grabs my wrist. I look into his eyes and they're apologetic, but there's still a little heat in his gaze as he shakes his head. "You're not a noisy eater. Let's just say that the sounds of you enjoying yourself are a little…" He looks up at the ceiling and takes a deep breath. It rushes out of his lips before his eyes meet mine. "Distracting," he says, his voice a little raspy.

"Oh." *Oh.* My eyes widen and I feel my cheeks heat again. I try to suppress the smile that threatens to take over my face, but it's difficult. I was turning him on, and the knowledge that I'm turning on a sexy man like Noah is all kinds of thrilling. I have some experience with men, but not a crazy amount, so this new bit of information is a nice ego boost.

He picks up his fork to continue eating. "Yeah, oh," he says, shaking his head at me good-naturedly.

I take another bite of food and seriously consider moaning again just to tease him, but I refrain. No need to torture the poor guy. After I swallow, I put my fork down and change the subject to a safer topic. "So, I haven't done much with the house other than paint a few rooms and replant the garden in the back. Like I said, I don't know much about this kind of thing and I can't afford a contractor. What do you think we should work on today?"

He finishes his last bite, pushes the plate away, and places his forearms on the table. They are sinewy and sturdy and I want to do nothing but hang off them like a sloth all day long, but I try not to let myself get too distracted and move my eyes back up to his. His smirk tells me he knows I was checking him out, but he doesn't say anything about it. "Well, Caity. This is your project, what's your main goal?"

"Well, I want to fix it up so I can resell it and possibly make a profit." Then I can take the money and travel or move around. I can do whatever I want. My parents are still in Sacramento with my brother, but I'm not close with any of them and don't feel the need to live nearby. They're all about socializing with the right people and status symbols like fancy cars or a nice, big house. That's never been important to me and won't be anytime soon. They consider me the family oddball, and I'm okay with that for the most part. I don't really know what I want to do to be honest, I just know that flipping the house is probably the smartest move.

"So, you don't want to live here yourself?" Noah looks a little dismayed at that. I'm not sure why, so I ignore it.

"Well, I guess not. I figured that trying to flip the house was the wise thing to do. I don't really have any plans long-term. I would like to settle down somewhere, but I'm not sure if that's here, or back in the city, or somewhere else entirely," I admit with a small shrug.

He brushes the back of his knuckles over his stubble and I can tell he's thinking about something. What that something is, I don't know, so I take the opportunity to finish my food. After a minute, he comes back to our conversation. "I tell you what. We're going to fix the place up, but in a way that you would be comfortable and happy if it were your forever home. Then, when that's all done, you can decide if you want to sell. Sound good?"

That does sound like a more practical plan, so I nod my agreement. "Yeah, I think that works for me."

"Excellent." He rubs his palms together and smiles. "Let's say I clean up the dishes and then you can give me the grand tour. We can decide what still needs to be done and where to start after I get a good look at everything." He stands and gathers our empty plates, moving toward the sink.

"Oh, I can do those." I start to stand and he comes over and gently pushes on my shoulder to put me back down.

"Don't worry about it, sweetheart." I smile at another new endearment and watch him work, wanting to just sit and do this all day. I startle at that thought, realizing that I'm starting to fall for him again already and it hasn't even been two full weeks. This isn't good. I don't get much time to think about that, though, because Noah finishes the dishes quickly and comes back over to the table.

He holds his hand out to me. "Shall we get started?"

I place my hand in his and try to ignore the warmth in my chest and the sheer sense of rightness that's flowing through me as our skin touches. "Let's do this," I tell him, and as we walk through the house hand in hand, I wonder if I wasn't talking about more than just home renovations.

Chapter Twelve
Noah

The students file into the library and make their way to the computers. I emailed Caity yesterday to see if the lab was free, and once she replied with a "yes," I booked it for one of my freshmen classes. I'm having them write a biographical essay on their favorite female athlete or sport, and while yes, there are other computer labs on campus, I wasn't about to pass up another opportunity to see my girl. It's been two weeks since I went over to her house, but other than letting me bring her coffee and help with remodeling, I haven't made much headway. I keep asking her to dinner and she keeps coming up with excuses to decline. She's still unsure about me, and while I understand the reason, I'm not necessarily loving the limbo we seem to have found ourselves in. We spent more than ten years apart and I don't want to waste any more time. I want to move forward.

My eyes roam the library until I look over at the half-moon circulation desk and see Caity speaking with a student. When she spots me, she smiles and holds up a finger to let me know she'll be with me momentarily, so I head up to the front row of computers and raise my hands to get the boys' attention in the meantime. They quiet down quickly enough and once all thirty-five heads are pointed my way, I start to explain their assignment. "All right, kids. Today you'll be researching a female athlete or sport of your own choosing and writing up a three-page biography or history of the sport. If you have any questions, either I or Ms. Walsh will be able to help you. Now, anyone need anything before we get started?"

Tommy Callahan raises his hand, so I nod at him. "Why do we have to do a female athlete? I don't even know any," he says with a grimace.

I point my finger at him and the rest of the kids follow the motion. "Well, Tommy, that's the exact reason why I am having you research it. Despite the fact that they're just as skilled, if not more so, than their male counterparts, female athletes don't get the same media attention or accolades that male athletes do and we need to change that. Now, if you need some ideas I would be happy to help you out, but there's also this little thing called Google. I suggest you use it." I look over the sea of teens staring at me. "Any other questions?" I'm met with nothing but shaking heads and light complaining about the assignment, so I move on. "Get to it, then."

The sound of keyboards clacking away starts up as I walk around the kids, making sure to answer questions and check their monitors to make sure they're working on the assignment and not just messing around on the Internet or playing solitaire. That's probably what I would have been doing in high school, and I chuckle at the thought. Now I'm the one trying to keep kids focused and I wonder if any of my old teachers would be horrified at that fact. I continue making my rounds when I feel a warm hand on my shoulder. I turn around and see Caity smiling at me. She's in burgundy slacks and a sleeveless, green blouse that shows off more of the creamy, white skin I want to pepper with kisses. Her hair is down again and every time I see it this way, I'm tempted to run my hands through it and see what she does. She's as pretty as a picture and I smile at her in return. "Hey, there."

"Hi," she whispers, and not because we're in the library. She's still a little shy around me every now and then, especially when other people are around, and I suddenly wish someone would pull a fire alarm so all these kids would beat it and we could have some alone time. I want her to open up to me again more than I've wanted anything in a long while, maybe forever.

"How are you today, darlin'? Did you get my present?" She was busy helping Mrs. Shen pull some books for her class when I came by to drop off her coffee this morning. In addition to the drink, I plopped a blueberry muffin and a Lego Batman keychain on her desk.

"I did, thank you. The coffee and muffin were delicious, and I already have my house key on Batman. He's currently patrolling the dark streets of my purse as we speak." She's close and it would be so easy for me to wrap my arm around her shoulder and tuck her right under my arm. She's the perfect height for that and I long for the day I'll be able to do it.

"Well, let's hope he's up for the job. I hear purses can be dangerous places and I'm not sure he can handle it. Maybe we need to call in some backup. Who do you think? Doctor Strange? He's good in dark dimensions." I snap my fingers. "No, I know. Ironman." She always got annoyed when I would say Ironman was better than Batman.

She slaps my shoulder. "I am offended at that implication. You know how I feel about Batman. He's my ride-or-die superhero," she says with a curt nod.

I chuckle. "Why is that again exactly? I'm not sure you ever told me."

Her face gets serious and she keeps her voice low so the conversation stays between the two of us, and I can't help but feel a little zing of pleasure at that fact. "Well, other than him being the world's greatest detective, he is computer savvy and can engineer just about anything, he's a trained ninja, and he has enough wealth to fund his crime-fighting and give to charity.

He's basically the whole package and his growling voice in the animated series is sexy as hell too."

"You really think his voice is sexy?" This is interesting information. I will shred my own voice box if it means I can make a sound that turns her on.

"Oh, totally. That voice could melt butter." She playfully fans herself and I smile.

"I don't know, darlin'. All that was convincing, but I think we're going to need to call the experts." I clap my hands to get my students' attention. "All right, listen up. Ms. Walsh and I need you all to settle a debate between us. Who is the better superhero: Ironman or Batman? Raise your hands for Ironman." About a dozen hands go up. "Okay, what about Batman?" More hands shoot up and I look over at Caity who is giving me a triumphant look. I scowl at my students. "Everyone who voted for Batman just failed the class." A few of them gasp and some chuckle. I wave off my comment and smile. "I'm just messing with you guys. Get back to work."

Caity leans back over to me "I'm always right when it comes to superheroes," she says in her singsong voice.

"Mmhmm. Say that again the next time you try to convince me that Aquaman isn't the worst superhero known to man," I retort, thinking I just won our little debate.

Her eyes narrow. "One word: Inhuman."

"Touché," I mutter and I hear her chuckle as I move around the room to answer some questions. I'm happy to be wrong if it makes her laugh and smile the way she is now.

The rest of the period flies by and the students need a lot of my attention, so I don't get many more opportunities to talk to Caity. We were back in our old rhythm for a moment there, and I want to keep that going as much as I can. I look up at the clock and see the bell is about to ring. I tell the kids to pack their stuff and turn off the computers before I head over to Caity. "Hey. Have lunch with me today?"

Her eyes widen. "Where? Here?"

"Here, outside, in my office, or in the cafeteria, I don't care. Hell, I'd climb up onto the roof and bake in the sun if it meant I got to spend more time with you," I admit. I would do just about anything for her.

She smiles sweetly at me. "Okay. How about we eat in my office. I don't want to bake in the sun, and no matter what you say, I know you don't either."

I chuckle and the bell rings. I wave goodbye to my students before turning back to Caity. "Let me grab my lunch out of the staff room and I'll be right there." She nods and I take off in a fast walk.

Luckily, the staff room is right near the library and I make it there in less than a minute. I head over to the fridge and see the flyer for the staff talent show on the front, shaking my head at the sight of it. You would never catch me up on stage in front of the entire school making a fool of myself. Every year the senior class picks a charity and the teachers sign up to showcase their talent in hopes of drawing enough people to buy a ticket in support. Some of the teachers are actually pretty good. The music, dance, and drama teachers are all fine and even a couple of core subject teachers can sing or dance, but most of the time it's a parade of teachers who do it simply for the laughs it brings to the students. Not me, though. I would not enjoy getting up on stage and making a spectacle of myself.

I open the fridge and grab my club sandwich and pasta salad before heading back to the library. Once I'm in I head straight to the office, stepping into the doorway and seeing that Caity has put down some napkins to form a tablecloth over the spare table and has pulled in another chair for me. I smile at her adding a few small details, and find that her treating this somewhat like a real date is promising.

Plopping down in the chair across from her, I watch with rapt attention as she unpacks her lunch bag even though it is one of the most mundane tasks known to man. She pulls out a PB&J sandwich, a little storage container of cut fruit, and a bag of what looked to be homemade chocolate chip cookies. She catches me staring and shrugs. "What can I say? I have a very sophisticated palette."

I gesture to my own lunch. "No judgement here. It's not exactly five-star cuisine on this side of the table." I grab my sandwich and take an exaggerated bite and it earns me a laugh. "Dig in," I mumble around the large bite. Caity continues to chuckle as she tears pieces off her sandwich. I noticed she eats almost everything in a similar manner and did so even in high school. "Why do you do that?"

Her hand pauses with a bite of sandwich about halfway to her mouth. "Do what?" she asks, looking slightly self-conscious.

"Tear into your food with your hands. I don't think I've ever seen you bite right into anything," I tell her. She always eats like a little bird, and it's endearing.

"Oh." She lifts a shoulder. "I had braces in junior high and I couldn't bite directly into anything without it getting all stuck in the wiring, so I started doing this. I guess it stuck." She pops the bite into her mouth and chews.

"Hmm. I didn't know you had braces." I take another bite of my sandwich and wonder what else I never knew about her.

"It's not a big deal. I'm sure there's lots of stuff you don't know about me," she says nonchalantly.

Hearing her say that has my hackles rising. I don't like that, not one bit. "I know enough, but I want to know more. I want to hear everything there is to know about you," I say adamantly.

We eat in silence for a few minutes and I wonder if she's going to address what I just said. Finally, she finishes her sandwich and dusts the crumbs from her hands. "I don't think you really want to know everything, Noah."

"Of course I do," I tell her. I want to know everything, from what her hopes and dreams look like to what brand of toothpaste she uses. No detail is too small or insignificant when it comes to her.

Her expression hardens. "Really? You want to hear about how lonely it was to grow up with parents who loved you *despite* the fact that you were so different from them? And on top of that, to not really have many friends?"

"Caity..." I start but she holds up a hand.

"Or should I tell you about how I was so messed up after what happened in high school that I never trusted my own feelings or the feelings of others? I dated a guy for over a year, Noah, and not once did I think he would ever choose me over someone else." Her eyes get a little misty, but she takes a deep breath and continues. "I don't blame you for my inability to trust other people. That started long before high school, but I let that hurt simmer for too long before I really looked at it and figured out I was part of the problem. I've worked on my self-esteem and I'm in a good place right now. All this ... us," she says fiercely, gesturing between the two of us. "It's just bringing things up again, old hurts and feelings. I just don't know what to think."

I move my chair closer to her and grab onto her hand. It's soft and a little calloused from all the work she does carrying and shelving books all day, but it's also solid and strong. That's what I need her to be right now because I can't lose her again. I want to hold onto her forever. I run my thumb across the back of her hand and look her straight in the eye. "Don't overthink this, Caity, please."

She sighs and leans back in her chair. She doesn't take her hand away from me and her expression softens a bit, and I take it as a good sign. I continue to move my thumb back and forth over her smooth skin, hoping to ground her and soothe her frayed edges. "I'm not so sure that's possible, Noah. All I do is overthink when it comes to you."

I lean in closer so she can see the sincerity in my eyes. "I won't hurt you again, Caity-bug." I take her hand and place it over my heart, covering it with my own. My heartbeat is steady and I wish she could be as confident in me as I am in her. "I swear to you, darlin'. I'm not that guy anymore."

Her chin wobbles and I push back the emotions that threaten to overcome me as well. "I know that, Noah. I know you're not that same boy who hurt me all those years ago. I know that up here," she says pointing to her head. "But I'm not so sure I feel it here." She moves her hand to cover her own heart.

I press my hand down onto hers and make sure she can see the fiery determination in my eyes. "I understand, but I'm not giving up. I'm going to make sure you understand it both up here…" I lightly brush my hand over her hair and then slowly move it down her cheek and neck until it's over her heart. "And in here." I lift her hand from my chest and kiss the back of her knuckles. A small tear escapes her eye and I brush it away with my thumb before clasping her cheek with my hand, sighing with relief when she leans into the touch. Part of her still wants me, and that's the part I need to reach. "I'm going to prove it to you. Don't give up on me, darlin'."

She leans further into my touch and places her hand over my own. "I don't want to," she whispers.

"Then don't," I plead. "Please." I will get down on my knees every damn day if I have to, and beg this woman to never give up on me. She finally nods and I breathe a sigh of relief. "That's all I ask," I tell her before leaning down to kiss her forehead.

I grab her hand again, intertwining her fingers with mine. Her head leans on my shoulder and while I savor the feeling, inside I am once again cursing myself for being such an idiot in high school. We sit in silence, knowing not much more can be said and I just want to let her relax after having to once again deal with the past. I'm still holding her hand and occasionally giving it a squeeze to let her know I'm here for her. When I feel a small squeeze back, I know we're okay, but I want us to be better than okay. I use the rest of our time together to form a plan. The small gestures aren't working and I realize I need to go big. I think back to the flyer on the fridge in the staff room and suddenly I know what to do. She put herself out there with that letter, and now I need to do the same. Let's just hope my guitar skills are up to the challenge.

Chapter Thirteen
Caitlin

This week has dragged and I'm ready for it to end, but I have to head over to the auditorium in a few minutes to sell tickets for tonight's "talentless show." That's what the staff have been calling it, and I feel bad that the ones who signed up have to hear it called that. I saw the dance teacher, Charlotte, practicing her routine when I walked by her studio the other day and she looked amazing, so poised and graceful. I could never put myself in front of a huge crowd like that and I have massive respect for anyone who does, regardless of whether or not they have skill. I just gave a boy a letter and it nearly ruined me, so I can't imagine what would have happened if I did some big gesture in front of a whole group of onlookers and it went bad.

Thinking about the letter again has me thinking about Noah. Our lunch last week didn't necessarily go smoothly, but I'm hopeful about the future. At least, a part of me is and I wish I could get my head and my heart in sync. After we finished lunch holding onto one another, he asked for my phone number. He could have just gotten it from the staff directory, but I appreciate that he wanted to get it from me. He's come by the library every day and calls me every night before I go to bed. We talk for at least an hour and fill each other in on the parts of our lives we didn't know and what we've been up to since high school. I heard all about his time at college and how when he got injured playing football, he found out who his real friends were, and it turns out there weren't many. Noah seems to have really grown and matured over the years and he's found his place here in Sun

Valley. I'm proud of and happy for him.

For my part, I told him more tales about growing up as the quirky nerd in a family of beautiful, social people. He listened as I complained about my lonely childhood and how I thought that would change when I was ten and my parents had another baby. It did for a while, but as soon as my brother was old enough to parade in front of their rich friends, they shuttled him around and bragged about how handsome he was and what a natural little athlete he was turning out to be. After that I talked about my life in the city and how I loved being able to go for nightly jaunts around different neighborhoods to check out various bookstores and eateries. I miss that part the most because I really hate driving, preferring to get outside and move around myself. When I told Noah that, he offered to shuttle me around so I never had to drive again and I laughed, but I believe he would do that. I'm starting to believe a lot of things he tells me. I'm still afraid of getting hurt, but I don't want to miss out on something wonderful because of that.

My eyes wander over to the clock and I see it's time for me to go. I exit the building and although it's finally fall, we're still in California and the night air only contains the slightest chill. Still, I'm glad I grabbed my sweater since I'll be in the auditorium under the arctic blast of the air conditioner. As I make my way over to the ticket booth, I see Gabe Hernandez setting up the cash boxes. Amelia is at his side, happily chatting away at him. When she sees me walk in, she jumps off her stool and heads over to me. "Hey, Caitlin. How are you doing tonight?" she asks politely, a bright smile on her face.

"I'm good. How are you?" I notice her baby bump is just the slightest bit larger and she rubs it gently.

"Oh, I'm pretty good. Now that the morning

sickness is gone, being pregnant isn't so bad. In fact, it has quite a few perks." She leans in closer to me. "My orgasms are so much more intense and I'm horny all the time, so we're having sex like three or four times a day," she blurts out to me.

I chuckle at her confession. While sharing that little tidbit, Amelia also neglected to lower her voice and I hear Gabe choke and his cheeks turn red. "Um, yes, it also seems to have affected her ability to filter information for what is and isn't appropriate to share at work." He gives her a pointed look as she smiles at him sheepishly.

"Sorry, hon. I'll try not to embarrass you again," she tells him. She bites her lip and he sighs, coming over to kiss her forehead.

"Don't worry about it, *querida*." He turns to me. "Now, did Sharon talk to you about how the cash box works?"

I nod and try not to look at the vice principal any differently, even though I now know way too much about the man's stamina. "Yup. They give me cash and I give them a ticket. I can make change, but no bills larger than twenty and no credit cards." Seems simple enough.

"Exactly. There's usually a bit of a crush at the beginning, but Amelia will be in here with you and I'll be outside wrangling the masses. Hopefully it goes smoothly and after a while, you should both be able to go in and enjoy the rest of the show." He hands each of us a key to a cash box and gently kisses his fiancée on the lips before he exits the ticket booth.

I sigh. "You guys are sweet," I tell her. I hope I have what they do someday. I think I could have that with Noah if I could just get past all these dumb insecurities.

"Thanks, but it wasn't always so sweet. I had to practically beg him to date me and even then, he got spooked once and we broke up for a few weeks. It all worked out in the end, but we had to sort out our own issues too," she explains.

I smile. It's good to know that not every couple comes ready-made and it gives me hope for my future with Noah. I nudge her with my elbow. "And now you get to have sex all the time."

She laughs and does a little happy dance. "Yes, I do!"

The gates shoot up and I see Gabe on the other side of the sales window. Amelia blows him a kiss and he winks at her before stepping into crowd-control mode. There are quite a few people waiting to buy a ticket and I feel a little nervous for all the performers. I was told it's more for laughs than anything else, so maybe it won't be that big a deal to the people on stage. I would be a wreck, though, and I'm glad I volunteered for ticket duty before someone tried to talk me into doing a skit or something.

Amelia and I sell tickets as quickly as possible to get everyone through the door and after twenty minutes, almost everyone is in their seats and ready to enjoy the show. We are in the booth for another fifteen, selling a few tickets now and then to the stragglers, when Amelia slides out of her stool again. "Can you watch the booth for a minute? I want to watch Madi and Owen in the English Department skit."

"Sure thing," I tell her and watch as she bounds out the door and into the main room of the auditorium.

I pass the time listening to the chatter and music that drifts into the booth from inside. I have no idea what they're doing, but there is a lot of laughter, so it's either really funny or really embarrassing. I hear a large round of applause and a minute later, Amelia pops back into the booth with tears in her eyes. "Oh my gosh, that was great." She's still laughing a little as she continues. "They all dressed up as each other and did impressions. Watching Madi and Owen imitate one another was great, but the best part was when one of Owen's fake boobs popped," she stutters out while laughing harder. "I told him not to use balloons." She wipes more tears out of her eyes.

I smile at her joy. "I'm sorry I missed that one."

She pulls her phone out of the pocket of her maternity dress and waves it at me. "Don't be. I'll text you the video." She starts typing away at her phone and I hear mine chime.

"Thanks for that." I grab my cash box and lock it up tight. "I think I'm going to head out. Want me to take your box up to the office for you?"

Amelia's face sobers quickly. "You can't leave. You haven't seen any of the show."

I shrug. "I'm good. I don't really enjoy the feeling of secondhand embarrassment." There's a reason I watch television shows like *Sherlock* and *iZombie* and not *The Office*. Cringe humor makes me uncomfortable.

She grabs both cash boxes and puts them in a file cabinet. "I promise you won't feel any embarrassment," she says confidently before grabbing my hand and leading me out the door. Next thing I know we are in the auditorium. A math teacher is just finishing up his magic show, dropping a set of silver hoops on the stage as Amelia drags me down to the front row. She tosses a sign marked RESERVED onto the floor and pushes me in the chair.

"Whose seat is this?" I whisper-hiss at her. The magician is walking off stage and Principal Langley walks toward the mic at center stage and I start to stand back up, but Amelia pushes me down.

"It's yours. Now promise me you'll stay right there for at least the next five minutes." I open my mouth to object when she levels me with a look so fierce I practically wilt. She points a finger at me. "Don't make me bust out my crazy pregnancy hormones on you. You want everyone in here to think you made me cry?" She makes her lip wobble for dramatic effect.

Jesus. For such a sweetheart, she is ruthless. I hold up my hands in surrender. "Okay, okay." She nods curtly before walking over to the wall. She casually leans against it and signals with her fingers that she's keeping her eye on me. Yikes. I hope I never really piss her off.

Sharon Langely speaks softly into the microphone. "Next up for you, we have the guitar and vocal stylings of our very own gym teacher and varsity football coach. Please welcome to the stage Mr. Noah Hunter." She claps and walks off the stage as the audience applauses and hollers for Noah.

He slowly walks across the stage, dressed up a little more than normal, wearing jeans and a green button-down with the sleeves rolled up to his elbows. He carries a stool and an acoustic guitar out to the mic and sets it up right in front of me. He looks a little blinded by the stage lights and I wonder if he can see me. He glances over at Amelia, and when she gives him a thumbs-up, he nods and sits down on the stool.

Cautiously, he lifts one foot onto the bar of his seat and places the guitar on his lap. He clears his throat off mic before speaking to the audience, looking every bit as nervous as I feel. "Good evening," he says, voice shaking slightly. "I'm not normally big on singing in public, but you see, there's this woman I'm trying to win over, and I thought what better way than to publicly embarrass myself?" That remark garners a few laughs, but not from me. I know I'm the one he's talking about, but I can't believe he's really up on that stage. The laughter dies down and he continues. "I knew her back in high school, and like most teenage boys, I was a bit of a dummy. No offense, gentlemen." More laughter follows, but he doesn't stop. "I hurt this girl and I'm trying to convince her to give me another shot. Hopefully, when I'm through, she'll know just how sorry I am and how much she means to me, has always meant to me. This is for you, Caity-bug."

He stops talking and takes a deep breath before he begins playing the opening notes to a song that sounds super familiar. I listen to the chords and try to place the tune. He leans into the microphone and starts signing. The lyrics are about being glad to see someone after so long, and I try to think of where I've heard them before, but I get too lost in his voice to properly place them. His voice is just the slightest bit gravelly, but it's really good and I shouldn't be shocked that Noah Hunter is also a very gifted musical artist. He keeps singing and it finally hits me that he's singing Taylor Swift's "Back to December." This song is so heartbreaking and I can feel that coming through in his voice. The lyrics go on to detail how the singer broke the heart of the person they loved and how they think back on it with regret. He continues to sing his heart out and when he get to the chorus, it hits me just how remorseful he really is about what happened between us.

I still don't know if he can see me beyond the stage lighting, but he's looking right at me and I hope he can feel my gaze on him. I'm mesmerized, unable to take my eyes off him. He's on stage pouring his heart out to me just like I did in that letter. I can feel the tears streaking down my face, and I don't even bother to wipe them away because this time they're tears of happiness, hope, and love. I told him in that letter that I would always love him and I meant it. I just buried those feelings and held onto the hurt instead, but no more. I'm not going to waste another minute dwelling on the past and what did happen, and instead focus on the future and what could happen if I just gave him another chance. Gave *us* another chance.

The song is starting to wind down and I bolt from my seat, not wanting to be apart from him any longer. I pass Amelia who is now joined by Madi, Owen, and Gabe, and they all smile at me as I rush by. I run up the ramp to the backstage area as I hear Noah finish the song followed by a crazy amount of clapping and whooping from the audience. I would join in but I'm too busy bobbing and weaving through curtains, props, and other performers. When I finally break free of the crowd and see Noah putting his guitar away, my heart stutters at the sad look on his face. Knowing I can wipe it away, I walk up behind him and tap his shoulder. He turns around and smiles hesitantly when he sees me. "I thought you left," he chokes out.

I shake my head. "No. I came back looking for you." I grab his large hand and hold it in my smaller one. "Did you mean it?"

He doesn't have to ask me to clarify. "Of course I did, darlin'. I was a dumbass to ever let a girl like you slip through my fingers, but one thing I do is learn from my mistakes and I'm not losing you again."

"You won't." I tell him, feeling hypnotized by the gaze of his hazel eyes.

He breathes out and swallows thickly. "You mean that, Caity-bug? You'll really give this a chance?" His expression is hopeful and I'm so happy to lean into that hope for both of us.

I take his hand and bring it up to my cheek. "I do mean it, Noah. I feel you here." I lightly press his hand into my cheek before dragging it down to cover my heart. "And I feel you here."

His brilliant smile seems to light up the entire auditorium and he scoops me up into a great big bear hug. He spins me around a few times and whoops in delight. Another teacher shushes us and he stops spinning and puts me back on the ground, but his smile is still wide and his eyes sparkle with joy. "Have dinner with me?"

Wrapping my arms around his waist, I hold him close and breathe in all the possibilities ahead of us along with his comforting, woodsy scent. Leaning my head on his chest and feeling his strong arms around me, I sigh and revel in the feeling of being close to the man I've always wanted but didn't think I could have. "I thought you'd never ask."

Chapter Fourteen
Noah

In hindsight, bringing Caity to The Posh Table for our first date probably wasn't one of my brightest ideas. It's crowded and I didn't think to call ahead and get a reservation. The hostess just informed me we would be seated in about two hours. This is the fanciest restaurant in Sun Valley, so I should have known a Saturday night would be busy, and while I'm glad I dressed the part in a pressed button-down and slacks, I still feel wildly out of place. Disappointed that our night will be on hold for a while longer, I make my way back to the sitting area where I left Caity and when I lay eyes on her, my feet stop in their tracks as I am once again taken aback by how gorgeous she looks. Her fiery-red hair is up and displays her swanlike neck, but there are a few tendrils loose that frame her oval-shaped face. She's in a red, spaghetti-strap dress and her black heels give her a few more inches, though she still doesn't reach my over six feet of height. Her emerald eyes snag mine as I approach and a wide smile pulls across her face. I'm glad she's happy, though I'm not sure how long that will last when I inform her we're going to be waiting forever to eat.

"Hey, you. Is our table ready?" she asks, her eyes sparkling up at me.

I scratch my jaw, missing the stubble I would normally find there. I'm clean-shaven tonight and between that, my clothes, and this restaurant, I feel nothing like myself, but I want to put my best foot forward with Caity. "Um. About that. Turns out this is the type of place where you make a reservation, but it didn't really cross my mind to do that." I brace myself for disappointment and frustration, but it doesn't come.

"Oh, no worries." She grabs her purse and slings it over her shoulder before she stands up next to me. "Where should we go instead?"

I stare at this amazing woman who couldn't care less that I am messing up the date she's been waiting over a decade for. "Um, we can go wherever you want, Caity-bug."

She taps her finger against her plump, red lips and I make a concerted effort to concentrate on what she's going to say and not how much I want to sink my teeth into her bottom lip. "I still don't know the area much and I've only been getting takeout from the Asian place down the street from my house." She grabs my hand and threads our fingers together. "Why don't you pick somewhere you're most comfortable? I don't need anything fancy, Noah. I'm not really a fancy person. I just want to be with you and don't care where that is."

I sigh. "Are you sure? I really wanted this to be special."

She tugs my hand and moves to the door of the restaurant, peeking over her shoulder at me and smiling brightly. "I'm with you, silly. It's already special."

I'm sure I have a dopey grin on my face as I look back at her as she leads me out of the restaurant. A fifteen-minute car ride later and we're sitting at a table in The Greedy Goat. It's busy, but there's a table for us and I know the food and service are on point. I pull out the chair for Caity and once she's sitting, I pull another chair up next to hers and put my arm around the back. She laughs and gives me a funny look. "What? I'm staking my claim. You look amazing and there are far too many men in this place, I don't trust 'em any farther than I can throw 'em."

She laughs. "You do realize that if someone did

try to pick me up, I would say no, right? This isn't the Stone Age and some guy isn't going to come up and club me over the head before dragging me back to his cave," she says, one eyebrow arched in amusement.

I scoot my chair even closer so our legs are touching and despite the warmth I feel radiating from her body, she shivers. Grazing my fingers over her shoulders, I smirk when I feel the goose bumps sprout up in their wake. I lean down, pausing near the base of her neck and inhale. She smells like something fruity I can't quite put my finger on, and I don't know if it's her perfume, shampoo, or just her, but it's driving me wild. Running my fingers over her creamy skin one more time, I whisper in her ear, keeping my voice low. "I'm not taking any chances with you, Caity-bug. I finally have you and I'm not lettin' go."

Her face turns toward mine and she looks down at my lips. I'm so tempted to kiss her, but I don't want our first kiss to be in a crowded bar. As if on que, our waitress comes over and I groan internally. It's Tiffani, and she's made it her mission in life to hit on me every time I come in here no matter how many times I give her the cold shoulder. Maybe now that I have a girl on my arm, she'll take the hint.

"Good evening," she says, digging around her apron for her notepad. I'm hoping she doesn't recognize me in my fancy clothes, but no such luck. She looks up and her face brightens. "Well, hey there, stud. It's about time you came back in to see me." I feel Caity shift away from me slightly as her body tenses, and I can't believe I messed this date up twice. She told me to pick somewhere comfortable and The Goat was the first place I thought of. I should have known better than to come to a pub where everyone knows me as a shameless flirt, even if that has never been the case with this gal in front of us.

"Evenin'." I keep it curt and tighten my arm around Caity even though she's still stiff as a board.

Tiffani clocks my movements, but doesn't let up. "So, what can I get you and your friend?" She heavily emphasizes the word "friend" and I'm starting to get angry.

"My *date* and I need a few more minutes with the menu if you wouldn't mind," I say through gritted teeth.

"No problem, baby. I'll be back in a minute." She trails a finger over my arm and I snatch it away. She doesn't care, though, and chuckles as she saunters away. I take a deep breath and turn to Caity who looks very uncomfortable.

"I'm really sorry about that, Caity-bug. I don't encourage her attention, but she likes to give it to me anyway."

She sighs and looks down at the table. "It's fine, Noah. I know you had a life before I came back and probably don't hurt for female attention," she says quietly.

I tuck my finger under her chin and pull her face up so she's looking in my eyes. "I did have a life before you came back, but it wasn't as good, and it never included her." I rub my thumb along her jaw, taking a second to enjoy the feel of her soft skin. "And the only female I want any kind of attention from is you. I'm a one-woman man, darlin'. And you're it for me."

Her eyes search mine for the truth and when she finally finds it, a small smile appears on her face. "Okay." I lean down and touch our foreheads together and breathe in her scent once more and that's when it hits me. She smells like strawberries on a warm spring day, and with her here next to me, I'm so happy I feel like I'm basking in the sun. Then I hear her whisper, "You're it for me too. Just so you know."

I lean back and kiss her forehead. "Glad that's settled then."

"Well, well, well. What do we have here?" Arthur Graham's booming voice cuts into our moment and I look up to see him smiling like a proud papa. "It's about time you cleaned yourself up and brought a date here. I'm offended you waited this long actually," he says haughtily.

I chuckle. "Sorry about that, Arthur." I sit back to make the necessary introductions. "Arthur, this is my girl, Caitlin Walsh. Caity, this is Arthur Graham, owner and proprietor of this fine establishment, as well as Amelia and Owen's father."

Caity holds her hand out to shake Arthur's, but he pulls her out of her chair and into a hug. "It's a pleasure to meet the lady who got this one to shave his face for once."

Caity hugs him back and laughs. "Oh, I wouldn't get too used to that baby face. I miss his stubble." She looks over at me, winks, and pulls back from the hug to rejoin me. "Oh, and I just love your children, especially your daughter. She is one of the sweetest people I have ever met."

"That's my sunshine," he says. "She takes after me, you know." He laughs and places his hand on the table. "Now, what can I get you two? I'll be taking care of you since your waitress is on break."

I say a silent prayer for mandatory work breaks and look over at Caty. "What'll it be, darlin'?"

She rubs her lips together as she considers the menu. "I'll have the fish and chips, please. And I'm good with water."

Arthur looks over at me. "I'll have my usual and a lager. Thanks, Arthur."

"Sure thing. I'll be back in a bit." He taps the table twice before heading back to the bar to place our order.

"He seems really friendly." Caity ventures.

"Yeah, he's great. He's kind of like a surrogate dad in a way." I haven't spoken to my dad in a few months and wonder if the next time we talk will be our annual awkward Christmas call.

"You and your dad still aren't close?" Caitlin grabs my hand that's not wrapped around her and holds it. I told her all about how my dad and I had football in common, but not much else.

"Yea. We don't talk often and when we do it's still mostly about sports. I'm good with it, though. Or, I guess I'm used to it now, so there's that," I say, a humorless laugh escaping.

She gives my hand a squeeze. "Well, at least you found a place where you belong. Your friends seem great and I've only known your surrogate dad for all of one minute, but I can tell he genuinely cares about you. It's nice."

I smile. "It is nice. What about your parents?"

She shrugs and her lightness fades. "Let's save that conversation for another time, maybe." She turns to face me a little. "Right now I just want to have fun with you."

"Sounds like a plan, sweetheart," I say with a smile.

"So, since you already got me out to dinner, does that mean you're done helping me with my house?"

Squeezing her shoulder, I pull her in a little tighter. "Oh, I don't think so. I'm going to be spending as much time with you as possible. After a few weeks, you'll probably be sick of me and need a break." I keep my voice light, hoping she won't hear the actual fear there. Or she'll decide I'm not worth the trouble and pull up stakes after she's sold the house.

"I don't think I could ever get sick of you, Cowboy. I plan on keeping you around for a long while." I can hear the sincerity in her words and it relaxes me some.

I look down at her and smile at my new moniker. "Cowboy, huh?"

She blushes. "I'm trying it out. You have a nickname for me after all."

"That I do, Caity-bug, and you can call me whatever you want. I'm yours." It's early days, hell, we haven't even finished our first date.

"And I'm yours," she tells me. My chest fills with joy at her words and I can't help the smile taking over my face.

Arthur comes back with our food and drinks and we speak with him for a bit and then continue to enjoy one another's company while we eat. By the time we get back to her place, it's late and I can tell she's tired. I walk Caity up to her front door and she unlocks it before turning around, looking up at me as she licks her lips. "Thank you again for tonight. I had a really good time," she says breathlessly.

I tug at one of the tendrils next to her face. "So did I, Caity-bug." I want to kiss her badly, the need to do it is coursing through my veins like wildfire and only the touch of her lips will extinguish it, but I want to do it properly and I need more than three minutes on the porch for that. Brushing the backs of my fingers along her cheek, I gaze into her gemstone eyes. "I want you to know something before I leave here."

"What is it?" She sounds concerned and that's the last thing she needs to be.

"I want you to know that I am going to give you a

very short, very gentle kiss on the cheek before I head back to my car. It's late and I know you've had a long week." I step closer and place one of my hands on the door behind her so she's bracketed by my arm. "But I also need you to know that I want to give you a proper kiss, quite badly. But when I get your lips on mine, I plan on taking my sweet time with you. You understand what I'm telling you, darlin'?" She nods and I lean down to lightly brush my lips against her cheek, struggling to pull myself away. When I pull back, I see they're now tinted pink and her eyes are hazy. "God, you're beautiful." I take a reluctant step back. "G'night, Caity-bug."

"Good night ... Cowboy." She smirks and heads inside. I turn around and stride over to my truck. Looks like the rest of my night will consist of a cold shower and a restless night's sleep, but I've never been happier.

Chapter Fifteen
Caitlin

The library buzzes with the sound of chatty students, and I'm so happy I've been able to create a safe haven for so many kids. As the weeks since the start of the year have progressed, I've had more and more kids come into the library in the mornings and afternoon to study, read, collaborate on projects with other students, and I even have a group that plays Dungeons and Dragons on Tuesdays right after school. They invited me to join, and I am seriously considering it.

Of course, the other reason I could be happy is that my first date with Noah the other night went so well. We hit a snag with the first restaurant and then with that annoying waitress, but after that it was smooth sailing. I reach up and touch my left cheek where he planted the lightest of kisses, wishing I could still feel his lips on my skin. I wouldn't have said no to a kiss on the lips, but he was right that I was tired. Besides, I am really looking forward to what happens when he takes his time. I've been dreaming of it every night since, and even the thought of it has me heating up. Fanning myself with a scrap of paper, I redirect my thoughts back to work so that I don't fall down a rabbit hole of erotic, Noah-centric daydreams.

The bell for class chimes and all the students scurry and leave the library quickly. I'm left alone once again, so I make my way back to my office, check my email, and finish the coffee Noah insists he still needs to bring me every day. I told him it was unnecessary, but he maintained that he wanted to spoil me and I didn't put up much of a fight after that. It turns out that I like being spoiled, though I have a feeling it's more about the man doing it than anything else. An email from Noah sits in my inbox and a small thrill goes through me when I click on it. He's asking if the computer lab is free third period and my mouth twitches at the corner, wanting to smile at the prospect of seeing him. When I look at my calendar, I am delighted to see that it is, so I shoot off a reply and spend the next two class periods anxiously awaiting his arrival.

The time drags until his appearance, but finally the door opens and Noah walks in carrying a rectangular box and a vase filled with some very unusual looking flowers. He is trailed by his freshmen PE class and they are all smirking at one another and giggling to themselves. "Get to the computers and get researching, boys. I need a moment with Ms. Walsh," he commands his class.

"You mean your girlfriend?" one kid asks with a snicker.

"Yeah, the one you sang to at the talent show," another chimes in with a laugh.

This feels eerily similar to when his friends made fun of me and even though they're just kids and I know they're not teasing me, I still feel a little uneasy and my chest tightens with anxiety.

"Of course that's what I mean. And I would sing her a thousand songs if that's what was necessary. Now get to work, you two," Noah tells the boys and laughs as he approaches me. The breezy way he just referred to me as his girlfriend and brushed off the jabs makes me feel so much better and the weight on my chest instantly disappears. He sets down his packages and picks up the small vase before handing it to me.

It's a ceramic vase, but it's in the shape and style of a book. It even has its own cover art. Inside are half a dozen paper roses and upon further inspection, I see that they're made from the pages of an actual book. His thoughtfulness has me floating on cloud nine and I can't stop myself from beaming up at him. "This is fantastic, Noah, thank you." I lightly touch the flowers and admire the craftsmanship. I love all things book related and have never seen a vase like this before. "I love the vase. Where did you get this?"

He scratches his cheek where his stubble is making a reappearance. I'm happy to welcome it back because it makes him look super sexy and I missed it. "Well, there's a little bookstore downtown where I bought the vase, and uh, I made the flowers," he admits, seeming just the slightest bit embarrassed. The tips of his ears turn pink and I can't believe this man's blushing. I love it.

"Well, they are the most beautiful flowers I have ever gotten. Thank you again," I tell him sincerely, squeezing his hand with mine for just a moment. Thanking him with a kiss would be a lot more fun, but we're at work, surrounded by students, and I want to hold him to his promise of taking his time with me.

He smiles softly. "You're welcome, darlin'." He picks up the box and passes it back and forth between his hands, looking a little nervous before finally blurting out. "Will you come to the football game Friday night? I have to coach, so I wouldn't be able to sit with you, but it would mean a lot to me if you were there," he asks. His expression is full of optimism and his hazel eyes bore into mine, pleading with me to say yes.

I smile at his nerves because it is the most adorable thing I have ever seen. This big, strong, handsome man is anxious for my answer, but he needn't be. As if I would ever miss an opportunity to see him. "Of course I'll be there. Thank you for asking me," I tell him as sweetly as possible.

He blows out a breath and I wonder if he thought I would say no. "No, thank you. And uh…" He hands me the box. "Wear this to the game, but wait to open it until lunchtime."

"Okay," I say, grabbing the box and holding it to my chest.

"Great." He hooks his thumb over his shoulder. "I should probably get back to doing my job now." He's all smiles as he backs slowly toward the rows of computers.

I chuckle. "Sounds good. I'll go put these in my office and come back to help you." I grab my gifts and head into my office, putting the flowers right where I can always see them and placing the box on my chair. I'm dying to open it now, but it can wait. I have something better than any gift waiting outside for me.

I spend the next hour helping Noah with his students and then the bell rings for lunch. He shuttles his kids out and I take the opportunity to sprint back to my office so I can open the box. With greedy fingers, I pick it up and place it on top of the spare table before hurriedly untying the big red ribbon that's wrapped around it. When I finally remove that and untangle myself from all the trimmings, I lift off the top. Inside is a bunch of tissue paper, but before I can move it Noah steps into the doorway and laughs. "Someone's an eager beaver," he says with delight.

I look up at him unashamed. "You said lunchtime and the minute that bell rang, it was lunchtime." Curiosity at what he could have given me is eating me up and my toes tap on the carpet impatiently as I wait to get back to it.

"That I did. Go ahead, darlin'," he says, tipping his head at the box.

I unfold the tissue paper and stare down into the

box. A small squeak of surprise bubbles up my throat. "Is this…?"

He nods and steps closer. "It is."

Gingerly, I lift Noah's high school letterman's jacket out of the box and run my hands over it. He didn't get a chance to wear it much in high school since it never really got cold enough, but when he did wear it, God, he looked like a teenage dream. I run my hand over the smooth, buttery leather and slightly pilled cloth material as I look at the different patches, and then turn it around to see the giant wolf mascot logo on the back. "Why are you giving this to me?"

He reaches out for the jacket and I hand it to him, gasping softly when he slips it over my shoulders and brings his hands and the sides together in the front. He holds the jacket closed with one hand and runs his other over a strand of my hair. "Because it's yours now. You're my girl, aren't you? So it's meant to be on your shoulders, not mine," he says reverently.

I look up at him and see a lot of genuine affection in his eyes. I really like being his girl and I like even more that he keeps finding ways to show how much he cares about me. I like that he always has his arm around me or that his name will be on my body, even if it's just on the outside of the jacket I'm wearing. I like him staking his claim and want him to do it often. "Thank you," I whisper.

"You're welcome. So, will you wear it on Friday?" The hope in his eyes is there again, and there's good reason for it to be. I don't think I'll ever say no to him.

"Just try and stop me, Cowboy. You're not the only one who wants everyone to know what this is," I say, swaying in place to show off my new threads.

"Oh, yeah, and what is this?" His eyes search

mine and I give him the truth.

"The beginning of something wonderful."

****

"These bleachers are so cold and uncomfortable," Amelia says as she squirms in her seat, trying to find a comfortable position. The bleachers are hard, the metal has only gotten colder as the temperature has dropped, and I can only imagine how uncomfortable they are to a pregnant woman.

"How about a nice warm bath and a back rub when we get home?" Gabe asks her, his eyes filled with adoration.

"Uh, that sounds like heaven. Can we go now?" Amelia is begging him with her eyes.

"There's barely any time left," Owen leans over and chastises her, a half frown on his face. "We're here to support Noah and the team."

"I know, but I want to beat the rush of people leaving," Amelia replies.

"Ugh, these nachos taste funky," Madi says. She sets them down on the bench in front of her and dusts her hands off on her jeans.

"I'll take care of those," Owen tells his wife before eating the rest of her food. He's already destroyed two hot dogs and his own nachos, so I can't believe he has any more room in his stomach. I've been too nervous to eat and had about a handful of popcorn before calling it quits. The rules are still foreign to me, but I know one thing about football that will always be true. It's better to win, and I want Noah to take his team to victory.

"It's almost over, *querida*. If you need me to, I will carry you out of here," Gabe tells her and she snuggles up next to him with a sigh. He really loves taking care of her, and I'm the teeniest bit jealous, but only because of how established their relationship is. Mine and Noah's is still new, and while I know it's heading somewhere great, I kind of want to hit the fast-forward button a little bit. Eleven years is a long time to wait to be with the man you love, and I don't want to wait anymore.

I glance over at the scoreboard. The Central High Bobcats are down by three. I'm not sure what any of the plays have been, but Owen and Gabe have been filling us in regularly. I've also been a little distracted because I've been keeping my eyes on the coach, spending as much time watching him as I have the rest of the game, probably more. He's wearing gray track pants and some kind of forest-green sports shirt. A ball cap covers his dark-brown hair, but every now and then he pulls it off to run his hands over his head in frustration. He also does a little fist pump when the team does well, and always gives the kids a slap on the back when they come off the field. It's obvious from the way he interacts with the kids that he really cares about the team. He clearly cares about the game too, but he prioritizes the players, not the score. I haven't seen him yell or get upset once. He gets discouraged, sure, but he never takes it out on the team. He's still the same boy I knew in high school, but he's matured and I can see it in how he interacts with the players, other coaches, and even the other team.

My gaze flickers to the time clock and it looks like there's only a few minutes left. I move my eyes from Noah to the field and try to focus on the rest of the game. The ball is hiked to the quarterback and he scrambles backward, dodging linemen as he moves. I watch another kid sprint toward the end zone and then the ball is sailing toward him. With more grace than I could ever muster, he catches the ball and crosses the line into the end zone where he does a victory dance. The Bobcats are now up by three and I jump up and down in my seat, unable to contain my excitement any longer. I'm not normally a sports person, but I'm so happy for Noah and his team.

There's just enough time left on the clock for the team to kick a field goal. It goes wide and misses, but it doesn't matter because they won the game. The team jogs in from the field and I witness Noah giving each one of them a slap on the back and what I know are words of congratulations. Even the kids who were on the bench for most of the game get some attention from him. After all the boys have filed out toward the locker room, Noah shakes hands with his assistant coaches before he immediately looks up and scans the already thinning crowd of fans. For a moment, I wonder who he's looking for, but his gaze finds mine and it stays there. He beams up at me and I smile, giving him two big thumbs-up. His smile widens at my dorkiness and he waves me down toward him.

"I'll see you guys later," I tell my new group of friends and start shuffling toward the aisle. I hear them all call goodbye and I should probably have stuck around longer for a proper farewell, but I want to get to my man. They're all loved up with their significant others, so I'm sure they get it.

Sprinting down the stands, I meet Noah at the bottom. I'm still a good three feet above him since he's on the field, but he doesn't seem to care. His hazel eyes twinkle as they shine up at me, looking just the slightest bit greener tonight, and I wonder if it has to do with the color of the shirt he's wearing or from the excitement and joy of winning the game. "Hey there, Caity-bug. My jacket looks good on you," he says with a slow grin.

My face heats with the attention he's giving me, but I preen as I twist side to side in his jacket. "This old thing?"

He chuckles. "Yes, that old thing. Thanks for coming tonight."

"Well, I had to come support my man, didn't I?" I ask, but I would have probably come even if he hadn't asked just for an excuse to see him again.

"Still. I appreciate it, darlin'." His straight white teeth gleam under the lights of the field.

I lean over the bar of the bleachers to get a little closer to him. "I do have a confession to make, though," I say, keeping my voice low as I look around like I've got some big secret. "I didn't follow much of the game."

"That so," he says with his lazy drawl and a smirk.

"Uh-huh. I was a little too busy watching the coach," I tell him with a little smirk of my own.

He grabs the bars and climbs up so that he's right in front of me now. I go to lean back a little, but he puts his arm around my back and keeps me where I am. I love the feel of his warm hands holding me close and I never want to leave the comfort of his embrace. "Well, this coach likes you watching him. In fact, knowing that is the highlight of my evening," he tells me, not an ounce of jesting in his voice.

"Even better than winning the game? Congratulations, by the way," I add belatedly.

He takes a breath and moves in even closer. "Thank you, darlin', and to answer your question, yes. Any attention I get from you will always be the best part of my day." He leans to the right and I feel the press of his warm lips against my cheek. My eyes drift closed and I revel in being his sole focus. When I open them again, I see Noah's smiling face in front of me. We hear his name being called and he looks over his shoulder. "I better go. I need to settle up here and make sure those boys aren't gettin' up to no good in the locker room." He leans back momentarily before closing in again. "I'm taking you out tomorrow morning."

"That so, Cowboy?" I ask, brow raised in question.

"Yeah, that's so." He jumps back off the stands and starts to move toward the breezeway, but before he gets there he turns around and gives me a nod and a wink. I raise a hand in goodbye and once he's gone I look around and see that most of the spectators have already left. Sighing happily, I walk toward my car with a big goofy grin. Everything between us is going so well and I am loving every minute of it. In fact, I think I might be falling in love with him again. The real, true, forever kind of love this time. And if I'm being really, really honest with myself, I'm just not falling, I'm pretty sure I already fell.

Chapter Sixteen
Noah

The cool morning air feels great in my lungs as I run laps around the track at the high school. I meet Owen here most weekend mornings for a run and this morning is no different, although he's wheezing and having a hard time keeping up with me today. It probably has to do with the earlier start time. I'm taking my girl out this morning and I wanted to squeeze in a run and a shower before I pick her up. Glancing over at my best friend, I chuckle softly when I see him dragging as we cross the lap marker. I turn and start jogging backward. "What do you think, four more?" I call out to him, a smirk on my face. He holds onto his side and flips me the bird. "Fine, pretty boy. Last lap," I call out with a laugh and turn forward again.

We finish up our final trip around the track and head over to the grass to cool down. I stand and stretch my arms over my head while Owen collapses onto the dewy grass and clutches his chest. "I ... shouldn't ... have ... had..." he wheezes out the words between breaths, "all ... those ... nachos."

I chuckle and stretch my quads next, enjoying the feel of the slight burn followed by the tension release. I can think of more fun ways to relieve tension, but I'm not sure how fast to move with Caity and I'm not willing to have her get spooked by me jumping the gun physically. I stretch out my calves next as Owen continues to catch his breath. I should have known he overdid it last night with the concessions. That boy hasn't met a food he doesn't like. Reaching out a hand to help him to his feet, I look at him with slight concern. "You okay, buddy?"

He takes my hand and stands, putting his hands on his knees. He's breathing a little easier now and his face is looking decidedly less purple. "I'm good, man." He stands up and takes a deep breath. "I think I need to up my cardio, though."

"You not getting cardio on the regular at home?" I ask, waggling my eyebrows. Owen punches my arm.

"One: none of your business what I get at home. Two: I get plenty." He smiles and looks around the empty track as if someone might be eavesdropping. "In fact, we're trying to get pregnant."

I smile. "Hey, that's great, man. I hope it happens for you guys." I know Madi especially has wanted to start a family for a while, so it's nice that her husband is on the same page.

"Thanks. I'm a little nervous, but I'm excited too. Plus, my mom would be over the moon if she got two grandchildren so close together. And she'll finally be able to extend her table," he says with a chuckle.

"Ha. I somehow doubt that would be the first thing on her mind." Owen and Amelia's mom, Sara Graham, was forever lamenting that she could never add a leaf in her table to make room for grandchildren. I guess it's finally happening for her.

"You'd be surprised. And if things work out for you and Caitlin, she'll have to bust out another leaf. She may pass out from all the excitement," he says, amused by his mother.

Picturing Caity and I spending time with our friend's family for holidays and other special occasions puts a dopey smile on my face. "That would be great. Let's just hope I don't blow it," I breathe out.

Owen frowns. "Why would you think you would blow it? You two looked pretty cozy after the game last night."

We were cozy and I loved every second of our short visit. "We're good right now. I've just never had anything this good in my life, so I'm kind of waiting for the other shoe to drop," I admit. My nerves sometimes get the better of me, but I'm trying to focus on Caity.

Owen claps my shoulder. "Don't overthink it, dude."

I nod and we start walking to the parking lot to grab our cars. "Such sage wisdom, my friend. Do all your students call you Yoda?"

He chuckles. "It is sage wisdom, and they totally should. If you need more of my wonderful insights, I'm here. Just remember you're a good guy, and she loved you once, yeah? I don't think it would be too hard for it to happen again."

"I suppose that's true." I try to focus on that fact and it makes me feel a little better. I stop outside my truck and pull Owen in for a hug. "Thanks, man. Have a good weekend."

He pulls away and raises his eyebrows. "I intend to. It's baby-making time," he says and turns toward his jeep.

"TMI, dude. Also, you might want to take a shower first," I tell him, wafting a hand in front of my nose.

He waves me off and gets in his car. I hop in my truck and head to my apartment to grab my own shower before taking my girl out for the day.

***

Caity opens the front door just as I raise my fist to knock. Her green eyes blink up at me from behind her glasses and I smile. I like that I can see her whole face when she's wearing her contacts, but I love seeing her in her glasses too. It's like looking at a living memory from the past, and I can't get enough of her. Her hair is down and a little wild today, sunlight catching on the occasional strand and lighting it up. I love her scarlet curls, like little rings of fire surrounding her lovely face. She's wearing a dark-blue sweater and jeans, both of which hug her lush body. She looks at my outfit and giggles. I look down at my own jeans and t-shirt and scowl. "What are you laughing at, Caity-bug?"

She continues to giggle and steps outside with her purse, locking the door behind her. "We match," she tells me, pointing between the two of us with her little finger.

I look again and she's right. We are wearing the exact same color top and our jeans are the same wash. Even our sneakers look similar. "Is that a problem? I can go home and change real quick if you want me to."

She shakes her head. "It's no problem, Cowboy. I just thought it was funny." She runs her hand up my arm and grabs my bicep. "Although, maybe you could lose the shirt for a little bit," she says, her pink tongue peeking out and teasing the corner of her mouth.

My eyes widen. Who knew little Caity Walsh was such a sassy flirt? "Oh, yeah. We're going out to some crowded places, but I'll forgo the shirt if you want." I make like I'm going to peel off my top and she stills my arms.

"Don't you dare, Noah Hunter." She grabs my arm and starts dragging me to my truck. "I don't want everyone seeing what's mine," she says, and the possessiveness in her tone has me smiling like a fool.

I stop and open the passenger door for her, helping her up and clicking the seat buckle for her because she's too distracted, her hand squeezing my arm as she feels me up. "Yours, huh?" I ask with a smirk.

Her hand stills and she looks into my eyes and

says firmly, "Mine."

There is fire in her eyes and I want to turn around and go straight back into the house, but I also want to do this right and show her how I feel with more than just my body. I've been that guy before, and I want to be more than that now. I know I am to her, but there's no rush here. I feel a rumble of pride in my chest at her words and a low growl comes out of my throat. "That's right, darlin'. I'm all yours." I shut her car door and round the hood to my side. Once I'm in, I buckle up and turn to her. "If you're good today, maybe I'll even give you a private show." I wink and start the car before pointing it toward downtown.

Ten minutes later, we're pulling into a spot right smack in the middle of Old Town Sun Valley. I thought Caity would appreciate the shops and cafes here since she seems to have an eye for small details and cute things. I hop out of the truck and get her door for her, gabbing her hand immediately and linking our fingers together. She smiles sweetly as I pull her toward our first stop. It's the coffee shop I've been getting her daily lattes from and I thought she might like to finally see it in person.

The aroma of roasted coffee beans and baked goods hits my face as we walk inside. The barista smiles at me and his eyes widen when he sees I have someone with me. Joe has seen me every morning for the last month and a half, and I'm sure he thought I was drinking two coffees myself because I always came in solo. "Well, well, well. Mister Black Coffee has a friend." He smiles at Caity. "Miss Vanilla Latte with a sprinkle of cinnamon I presume?"

Caity giggles and waves a little. "Um, yeah, that's me," she says, her cheeks getting a little rosy from the attention.

"So, the regular then?" Joes asks with a friendly

smile.

"Yes, same coffees to go, and a muffin. Which one do you want, darlin'?" I look over and her nose is already almost pressed up to the glass as her eyes scan the pastries on display. My girl loves her muffins and I am happy to provide for her.

"I'll have the pumpkin streusel, please." She starts digging through her purse and looks up at me. "I'm buying your coffee today, just so you know," she tells me, a playful look on her face.

"Fine by me, sweetheart. I never turn down a free meal." I smile at her and she hands her credit card over to the cashier.

Joe comes over with our drinks and food. "Here you are." He flicks his finger back and forth between the two of us. "I like this. You guys are cute, and I was seriously getting worried that you were over-caffeinating," he says, looking at me like I should be in the intensive care unit after all my coffee consumption.

"Well, now you know the real deal. Thanks, Joe." I wrap my arm around Caity and steer us toward the door.

Once we're outside, I snuggle her closer and take a sip of my coffee. "Thanks for the coffee, Caity-bug." I kiss the top of her head and get a hint of her strawberry scent.

"I figure it's the least I could do since you've been buying me one every morning. You should own stock in that place by now," she says with a light laugh.

I chuckle. "Who needs stock when you have a punch card? I get my money's worth on double-punch Wednesdays." She smiles and we chat idly about our weeks as we walk around the area. Spying the perfect place to take a break, I pull her over to a wooden bench under a tree so she can eat her muffin. "Let's sit a minute and you can eat your breakfast." I place my arm on the back of the bench in hopes she cuddles up next to me.

Caity sits down right where I was hoping she would, and I stretch my legs out and run my fingers through her hair while she tears little pieces off her muffin before popping them into her mouth. I love watching her eat. She's like an adorable little chipmunk. Her eyes wander the courtyard in front of us as she looks around and takes in the sights. "This is a really nice part of town. I'm surprised I haven't seen it until now."

"You never came down here when you visited your grandma?" I ask, curious to know more about the woman I am falling for all over again.

"No. We didn't really come visit her that often. We came when I was younger and I loved it. Gran would always be giving me books or letting me watch the cartoons my parents didn't approve of. How can you not approve of cartoon Superman?" She shakes her head and rolls her eyes. "After a while, we just stopped coming. Gran would come up to see us at our place in Sacramento, but we never came back down here. I think my parents thought this town was small potatoes or something since they've always been big city people. I thought that meant they would visit me more when I was in college and working at the library in San Francisco, but it didn't happen often," she admits. There isn't much sadness in her voice, just acceptance, and it breaks my heart.

"I'm sorry you grew up with parents who couldn't appreciate what a wonderful person you are." I give her shoulder a squeeze with my hand and tug her closer.

She lifts her hand up to mine and holds it there. "You too."

I smile sadly. Neither of us won the parent lottery, that's for sure, but neither of us has let it make us bitter, hard people, and for that I am grateful. "Thanks, darlin'.

Now, how about we finish up that muffin and I take you to a little bookshop?"

"What do you mean 'we'?" She eyes me skeptically as I reach over, nab a chunk of her breakfast, and pop it into my mouth.

Her jaw drops. "I would never have agreed to this date if I had known you were a muffin thief. I don't share food, Noah Hunter," she states firmly, poking me in the chest. What is it with women and that gesture?

I scoff, rubbing the spot she just assaulted. "What do you call the other night when you ate some fries off my plate?"

She juts her chin out defiantly. "That's different."

"How so?" I ask, my mouth pulling into a smile despite her not making a lick of sense.

"Because when I do it, it's cute and when you do it, it's rude," she says with a sweet smile.

I bark a laugh. "It is cute when you steal my food, but I'm not making any promises that I won't reciprocate."

"Fair enough," she mutters, dissatisfied.

I chuckle at her. "C'mon, Grumpy. Let's walk it off." I stand and help her to her feet. After tossing our trash, we walk around the main thoroughfare and go inside the little bookshop where I bought her vase. She buys a couple of romance books as well as an artsy bookmark. "You can never have too many," she told me. Then we stop in the comic book store for a while and get sidetracked talking to the owner about the Marvel Cinematic Universe, and Caity goes on a rant about how DC has better heroes, but crappier movie makers. We stop in a few other random stores and just browse and goof around for a few hours. It's like old times, only better.

We're just leaving a vintage clothing shop when I

hear her stomach growl. It has been a while since she had that muffin and I don't want her going hungry, but more than that I don't want this date to end. Grabbing her hand, I pull her into a small alcove away from the foot traffic. "Hey, how about we pick up some lunch on the way back to your house and I can help you with a few things?" I hope I don't need the promise of home renovations to earn an invite back to her place anymore, but you never know.

Caity gives me a knowing look. "I like that idea, but you don't have to help me with anything. We can just enjoy the day together."

Her sweet smile warms my chest and I would love nothing more than to just be with her, but I do genuinely want to help her with her goals. "Tell you what. How about we go out for lunch, and then pick up some supplies for dinner at the store? I'll help you move all that old junk out of the garage and then I'll make you dinner."

Her nose scrunches up adorably and her eyes narrow. "You don't have to do all that for me, Noah. You don't have to take care of me for me to want to be around you. Have I made you feel that way?" She looks distressed at that thought and I quickly assuage her fears.

"Not at all, sweetheart. I know you like me for me, but I happen to like taking care of you. It makes me feel good." It makes me feel like I'm the most capable man in the universe and I'm grateful she has let her guard down enough to let me take care of her.

She bites her lip, but releases it before I can do it for her. "Well, if you like taking care of me, far be it for me to deny you the pleasure," she says with a small shrug of her shoulder.

Looking down at her rosy cheeks and full lips, I start to rethink my position on PDA. No, it can wait, but I can still tease her a little. I lean down next to her ear, brushing the shell with my nose before whispering, "Oh, darlin', you haven't seen pleasure yet, but don't worry. You will." I brush my lips against her cheek as I pull back and see that she's now flushed from her hairline all the way down to her chest. I smirk. "Shall we?"

She nods and I pull her toward the car. Once she is safely inside, I adjust my pants and get into the driver's seat. Teasing her turned out to be a bit of a tease for myself. I know I thought that taking it slow was a good idea, however, right now I'm seriously struggling to see merits in my plan.

Chapter Seventeen
Caitlin

Watching Noah move boxes and random pieces of furniture to the back of his truck shouldn't be entertaining, but I can't seem to find the motivation to leave my spot leaning against the door that separates the garage from the house. His t-shirt stretches across the strong muscles of his back and every now and then the front rides up and I get a peak of his taut stomach and the line of hair that trails down into his jeans. I could watch him work for hours and not just because he is easily the most handsome man I have ever seen. The fact that he's helping me with the house, doing projects I already told him he doesn't need to do, just being here consistently is what makes him so sexy. I just wish he wasn't also being such a gentleman when it comes to our physical relationship.

I don't have a great amount of sexual experience, but I have missed being with a man. Being around Noah and not taking things further makes me feel like my insides are ready to boil over. I could handle waiting if he would at least kiss me, but he hasn't made a move yet and I'm thinking maybe he needs a little motivation. I start to form a plan and will set it in motion soon enough. In the meantime, I'm going to sit here and enjoy the show. I watch him move the last box into the back of his truck and he dusts his hands off. The weather is nice today, so he didn't really work up a sweat. If it was hot out, I bet I could have talked him into working shirtless, and I really want a glimpse at all the hard muscle and golden skin.

He shuts the door to the bed of this truck and

turns around. "Enjoying yourself there, Caity-bug?"

I smirk. "Oh, I am most definitely enjoying watching you work," I admit, unashamed that I've been ogling the man. Pushing off the door jamb, I walk over to him, wrap my arms around his waist, and lean my chin on his chest, looking up into his eyes with a smile. "Thanks for all your hard work, Cowboy."

He leans down and kisses my forehead. "Anytime, darlin'."

"Hmmm. I like the sound of having you here anytime I want." We've only been together for a couple of weeks, but I already want him around all the time.

"Well, you have me," he vows, kissing my forehead again and swaying me slowly from side to side.

I relax in his arms for a moment before pulling back. "All right, Cowboy. Time to head in and wash up for dinner." I make my way back into the house, Noah trailing behind me.

"I thought I was making you dinner." He pouts. I can imagine it's what he looked like as a little boy when he didn't get his own way, and the thought of us having a little kid just like that has me beaming over at him.

"Nuh-uh. You took me to lunch and cleaned out my garage. I now have a place to park my car and for that, I am going to make you dinner." I walk to the kitchen and shove him toward the bathroom. "Now wash up and maybe I'll be really nice and let you peel some carrots or something," I relent.

He mock-swoons. "Peeling carrots? My, my, Miss Caity, you sure know how to sweet-talk a man."

I laugh and give him another shove. He heads into the bathroom and I make my way to the kitchen to get the food going. I take out the skirt steak strips I started marinating when we got back and grab the peppers and onions as well. I'm cutting up the vegetables when I feel some hands gently grasp my hips and warmth pools in my belly. Noah leans down and rests his chin on my shoulder. "I thought I was peelin' carrots?"

I smile and tip my head so it rests next to his. "Not anymore. You did so well moving those boxes, I decided to upgrade you to guacamole duty."

He smirks. "Well, darlin', I sincerely appreciate your confidence in my ability to smash avocados. Where are they at?" he asks, looking around the small kitchen.

"They're in the fridge, but you don't have to get started just yet." I look at him and smile. "I kind of like where you are right now."

"That so?" he asks with a grin.

I nod and get back to chopping the veggies while I lean back into him. He is warm and the hard planes of his muscles should be uncomfortable, but I've never felt cozier or more relaxed. I finish my chopping and toss the veggies in the pan to cook before spinning around and resting my hands on Noah's chest. "I should probably let you get to work, or we won't be eating anytime soon."

"Eating is overrated," he says with heat in his gaze.

I reach over and flick off the stove. "It very much is." I lick my lower lip and he follows the movement of my tongue with his eyes. "You ready to take your time with me yet, Cowboy?"

He groans and rests his forehead against mine. "I've been ready for a long time, Caity-bug. I don't want to rush anything, though. You mean too much to me."

I smile and my heart soars with the admission. He means a lot to me too, and I appreciate that he wants to do things right, but it's time to throw caution to the wind. "I've been waiting almost half my life to kiss you, Noah Hunter. I'm tired of waiting."

His hands come up and cup both of my cheeks.

"You're sure?"

I barely start to nod before his lips are on mine. They are warm and full and feel so very right as they brush against my own. The kiss starts slow and gentle, but then I lick his lower lip and it's like a signal for him to unleash the beast. He tilts my head and his tongue makes its way into my mouth. He tastes spicy and sweet, like cinnamon gum or ginger snap cookies. I know for a fact he hasn't had either of those today, so I file that away as just being how the man naturally tastes, and I am already addicted to it. Our tongues dance and tangle as my hands move from his wide chest to wrap around his thick neck, playing with the short hair at the nape when I get there. I pull him into me a little more and I didn't think it was possible, but he deepens the kiss even more and I groan audibly. My body squirms against his as he continues to drive me wild with his attention. We take turns sucking on each other's tongues and are basically devouring one another. It's like he's trying to suck the soul out of my body and right now I would let him. He can have it, he can have all of me as long as he keeps kissing me like this. His hands coil into my loose curls and he gathers them together before pulling us apart.

"Goddamn, Caity-bug," he states as we both pant and catch our breath. "Just ... goddamn." He dives right back in and we're kissing again like our lives depend on it. My body sings as I slide my arms down his chest and wrap them around his back, using all my strength to pull his body closer to mine. I feel the evidence of his arousal hit my belly and I moan. He's not a small man and if I feel what I think I feel, that's true for all of him. His hands move down to rub my shoulders and even as he's destroying me with this kiss, he's taking care of me by easing my aches and pains. It's the most amazing kiss I have ever had. I can feel tingles all the way from the top of my head to the tips of my toes, and I never want it to end. I slide my hands down to his rear and grab on tight, squeezing the firm globes with all my might. He breaks the kiss and once again rests our heads together. "I'm going to have to ask you to stop doing that, Caity-bug. I'm barely holding on as it is."

I pop out my lower lip, but move my hands up to his lower back. "What if I don't want you to hold on? What if I want you to let loose?" I do, badly, and my lady parts are screaming at the two of us asking why we're wasting time in the kitchen when the bedroom is twenty feet away.

I'm pretty sure I hear a low growl come from his throat. "You are too tempting, you know that?" He licks his lips, but backs away and adjusts his pants. "I'm trying to do right by you, Caity-bug. I'm trying to prove that I'm a good guy."

I reach out and stroke his jaw, enjoying the rough feel of his stubble on my palm. "You don't need to keep proving yourself to me, Noah. I know you're a good man." I've known it for a while, and he proves it more and more with each passing day.

He closes his eyes and leans into my touch, bringing his hand up to hold mine against his cheek. Once he's taken a deep breath, his hazel eyes open and focus on mine. "I think maybe I still need to prove it to myself too," he admits, his voice trembling slightly.

I nod, understanding that it's important to him, and even though I've been waiting a long time for us to be together, I can wait a little while longer. "Okay. I can wait as long as you need me to." I lean up and lightly brush my lips against his. "But I still want some kisses every now and then, Cowboy."

He chuckles and kisses the tip of my nose. "Sounds good, sweetheart."

I smile up at him and roll my eyes slightly. I want a heck of a lot more than a kiss on the nose and he very well knows that, but I'll let it pass. "Smartass. Now, go smash some avocados," I tell him and smack him on the butt.

"Bossy," he says and starts grabbing avocados from the fridge to make the guacamole for dinner.

I get back to cooking veggies and the steak and we work in tandem for the next thirty minutes, chatting about everything and nothing. It all feels very domestic, and I can easily picture us doing this every night after work. Maybe I don't need to sell this house after all. Maybe I can make it a home with Noah. I brighten at that thought and once everything is cooked and the tortillas are warmed, I get an idea of how to make the evening even more enjoyable. "Dinner and a movie!" I blurt out.

Noah chuckles. "What?"

"Dinner and a movie. Let's watch a movie while we have dinner. I always thought it would be fun to watch a movie with you while we cuddled and ate on the couch." I smile a little sheepishly. "Probably pretty lame as far as fantasy dates go, but it's what I always pictured us doing when we were younger."

He smiles and grabs my hand, rubbing his fingers along the inside of my wrist. I shiver. Every one of his touches elicits a pleasurable response and I hope he realizes he's a good man soon, because my hormones are in overdrive. Until then, I'll just have to take what he's willing to give me. "It's not lame at all, sweetheart. It's what you always pictured, so let's make that little dream a reality."

I hum. "Thank you."

He smiles and we gather up our food and drinks and head to the couch. "What do you want to watch?"

"Well, since you are the guest, I should really let

you choose. I only have one request that it be a superhero movie." It's my go-to genre and it's a safe bet he'll enjoy it too.

"Is that part of your little fantasy?" He smirks, sitting down on the couch and placing his food on the coffee table.

I sit next to him. "Maybe." It's not the only thing that was part of that little fantasy. I distinctly remember in high school thinking about making out on the couch and possibly losing my virginity to the quarterback, but I tuck that tidbit away for later. I don't want to pressure him into anything he's not ready for.

"Well, then, how about we watch *Captain America*?" He reaches for my remote, turns on the television, and brings up my streaming service.

"Oooo. Chris Evans? I could watch him all day," I joke, changing a quote from the movie.

Noah's brow furrows. "Never mind that then, and that means we won't be watching *Thor* either because I'm sure you have a similar attitude about Mr. Hemsworth?"

I smile and shrug. "What can I say? He's super pretty." It's not a lie, and it's fun seeing Noah get all worked up.

He huffs. "What about a DC movie then. *Batman Begins*?""

"Mmm. Christian Bale," I say dreamily.

"*Man of Steel*?" he asks, playful irritation on his face.

"Henry Cavill in all his shirtless glory," I remark, basically just teasing him now. All of those actors are attractive, but none of them could hold a candle to him.

He growls impatient. "That's it." He starts scrolling through the list of movies and points a finger at me. "Just remember, you brought this on yourself."

I check out the screen and squeal with laughter as the title comes up. "*Howard the Duck*?" I continue to cackle. "How is this even available to watch?"

He laughs slightly. "I don't know and I don't much care, darlin'." He leans back on the couch and picks up his plate. He brings a fajita up to his mouth and goes to take a bite before he stops and glares at me. "You don't have a thing for talking ducks now, do you?"

I smile coyly. "Only Daffy."

He shakes his head and smiles before biting into his food. We spend the first half of the movie eating and poking fun at the ridiculous plot. It's fun and comfortable and exactly like I hoped it would be. After a brief intermission to clean up, we sit back down and I cuddle next to Noah, my side tucked right up underneath his, my legs draped over to the other side, and my head leaning on his chest. I can hear his heart beating and love that it's strong and steady, just like him. I wish he could see himself through my eyes. Yes, mistakes were made in the past, but he's learned from them and grown into such an amazing man. I cuddle in closer and let the constant beating of his heart lull me into a sense of comfort I've never known before now. I take a deep breath and close my eyes, just for a moment, so I can relish the feeling. It's not long before I'm so relaxed that I drop into a state of unconsciousness.

I slowly come back to myself and I can still hear Noah's heartbeat, but my body isn't sitting on the couch anymore, but being jostled gently. I'm pressed up against something solid and warm, and I feel weightless, like I'm floating through the clouds. I slowly blink my eyes open and see Noah lit up only by the small light coming from the living room. He's carrying me down the hall to my room and I shift so I can hold onto him. He looks down at me with a sweet smile. "Hey there, Caity-bug," he whispers.

"Hey." I'm a little groggy from my nap, but I am awake enough to be able to enjoy the feeling of being carried in the strong arms of my guy. "Sorry, I fell asleep."

We cross the threshold into my room and he goes to the side of my bed before lowering me down. I never made the bed this morning, so after I'm settled, Noah pulls my bedspread up to cover my body. He rubs my arm over the fabric and I wish he was climbing in next to me. I would love to spend the night wrapped up in the security of his capable arms. "Don't be sorry." He reaches up to tuck some stray curls behind my ear. "Awake, asleep, it doesn't matter. As long as you're mine, I'll take whatever I can get."

I hum, loving the happiness that spreads through me when he calls me his. "Thank you for this evening. I had a good time," I tell him, stifling a yawn.

"Me too, darlin'. Me too." He leans down and kisses my forehead. "I better go and let you get some sleep."

I pout. "I don't need sleep." I try to stifle another yawn, but it breaks through. "I'm totally awake."

He huffs a laugh. "Keep telling yourself that, sweetheart." He kisses the tip of my nose and then lightly brushes his lips across mine. "Sweet dreams, Caity-bug."

"You too, Cowboy," I say as I start to drift off again.

I feel the mattress dip as he gets off and heads toward the door, taking one last look at me. I think of all the wonderful times I have had with Noah so far and all the wonderful times we have to look forward to in the future, and I have very sweet dreams indeed.

Chapter Eighteen
Noah

The bell rings for lunch and I wave to my students as they rush off to refuel after having played racquetball for the last hour. I toss the balls and racquets in the equipment room for the next class to use and head back to my office, pulling the keys out of my track pants to unlock the door, but stop short when I see Caity leaning against the wall with a small cooler in her arms. She sees me and smiles sweetly, her cheeks turning the slightest bit pink and matching the blouse she's wearing. "Hey, darlin'. To what do I owe the pleasure?" I keep walking and unlock the door for my office and usher her inside. I take a seat at my desk and she plops down in one of the two chairs across from it.

"I missed you, so I thought I would come by and bring you some lunch." She holds up the cooler with a question in her eyes.

"That's mighty thoughtful of you, Caity-bug. Thank you." Her big smile is all the response I need and I clear some space on my desk for the food she starts to unpack. "You didn't need to bring me anything. I would have been happy with just you."

Her pink cheeks darken and she looks up at me with so much affection my heart aches. "I know, but I like doing things for you too."

She has no idea the things she does for me and to me. I've been in a state of almost perpetual arousal since our little makeout session in her kitchen and the one that followed the next day when I came back to help her power-wash her fence. It turns out most of her upgrades were just things that needed a good, deep clean and I'm happy she's saving money, but it also means she'll be done with the house sooner and she still hasn't told me whether she plans on staying in Sun Valley. That thought is enough to dampen the desire I feel when she's around. I don't want her to go, but I'm not sure we're at a place where I can ask her to stay.

"Speaking of which," she says as she pulls out Reuben sandwiches and broccoli salad. "I wanted to do something nice for you for all the help you've been giving me around the house." She takes an envelope out of her purse and slides it toward me. I get a vague sense of déjà vu. The last time she handed me an envelope, I broke her heart. I really hope that doesn't happen this time.

"What is this, darlin'?" I say, eyeing the small paper pocket and wondering what could be inside.

"Just open it silly." She smiles and I breathe a little easier. She seems excited, so I'm happy to oblige her. I pull out two tickets to the San Francisco 49ers game in two months. I look at the seats and they're really good. She must have spent a pretty penny on these and I am floored by the gesture. When I look up at her, she's biting her lip, nervous about my reaction.

"These are amazing, Caity-bug, but I can't accept them. I haven't done nearly enough work around your house to justify the expense." I really haven't done all that much. She repainted everything and retiled a bathroom floor before I got there. All I've done is clean up some old junk and wash a few things.

She comes around my desk and sits on my lap, her arms wrapping around my neck as she leans in close. "You've done a lot, Noah, and not just around my house. You've helped me heal a part of myself that I thought would be scarred forever. You've been nothing but attentive, generous, and caring. I wanted to do this for you. Please take the tickets," she pleads. She rests her head on my shoulder and rubs her hand up and down the back of my neck.

I stroke my fingers gently through her hair, processing what she just said. I guess I'm doing better than I thought and I don't want to hurt her by throwing her generosity out the window. "All right, but on one condition."

She tilts her head up and kisses my chin. "Name it."

"You come with me. We'll spend the weekend in the city, and you can show me all your old haunts before we go to the game Sunday night." I continue to stroke her hair and hope she takes me up on the offer. I haven't been back to the city in a long time and I would love to spend a weekend with her, seeing it through her eyes.

"Are you sure you wouldn't rather take Owen? Or Gabe?" she asks, her eyebrows pulling together in confusion. I would never pick anyone over her again.

"I would much rather go with you. Besides, if I take Gabe he'll fret about Amelia the whole time and Owen will eat all my food," I admit with a smile.

She giggles and moves to get up, but I grab her hips and pull her back down. I grab the food and scoot it closer to us. "I like you right here if that works for you."

She smiles at me and grabs a sandwich. "It works for me," she says before kissing my cheek.

We chat and eat for the rest of the lunch period and the time goes by way too fast. We're packing up the food when the bell rings and I wish I had prep this period so I could follow her back to the library like the little lost puppy I am whenever she's not around. She grabs the cooler and heads for the door, but I grab her arm and spin her back so I'm holding her. "I'm comin' over later, right? I want to spend more time with you."

"It's Thursday. Aren't you gaming with your friends?" I like that she knows my schedule well, but I also need her to know I'm making her a priority.

I shake my head. "Nope. They're all preoccupied and I want to spend time with my girl. I should be done with practice by five and will grab some food on my way over."

She leans up and kisses my lips gently. "I have a better idea. How about I come to your place and I bring the food?" she suggests.

She hasn't been to my place yet and for good reason. It's basically a series of white walls, a couch, and a bed. I'm not necessarily ashamed of my apartment, but it's not quite a home that she would feel comfortable in. "Your place has more room."

"I don't care. I want to see your space." She kisses me one more time before heading back toward the door. "Text me your address," she calls over her shoulder. My stomach drops as I wonder how much work I can get done before she gets there. Hopefully she won't see my bachelor pad and run the other way.

****

There's a knock at the door and I'm grateful for whatever delay got me fifteen minutes to make my apartment more presentable. It's still very much a sad shell of a home, but at least it's very clean. I walk over to the door and greet Caity who's standing on the doorstep looking adorable in her jeans and Superman hoodie. Her hair is in a low ponytail and she's taken out her contacts. "Hi!" She comes up and gives me a big hug. I automatically wrap my arms around her and back us inside. She giggles against my chest. "You trying to hide me or something, Cowboy?"

"Not at all, sweetheart. " I grab the takeout bags from her and place them on the kitchen counter next to me as I kick the door shut. "I just don't want an audience when I do this." I lean down and claim her soft, full lips. She tastes like strawberries and springtime and I wonder how she manages to both taste and smell like my favorite time of year. I hold her tighter and deepen the kiss, angling my head so I can sip from her mouth. She moans and her tongue dives into my mouth, gliding against mine. Her hands snake up behind me and she runs her nails down my back, causing me to tremble. I love it when this shy little thing takes charge and I love even more that I seem to be the one to bring it out in her, but I need to take care of her too, so I pull back just enough to nip at her bottom lip before I break the kiss entirely.

"I need to feed you," I tell her, my mind fuzzy with lust.

"I thought eating was overrated," she says, breathless.

I kiss her again, slowly, and more gently this time before I comment. "It is," I say once I'm done kissing her lips until they're red and swollen. "But I want to have some energy for you and I'm a little rundown from practice this afternoon."

She moves back, but I make sure she stays in the circle of my arms. "Why didn't you say so? I'm supposed to be taking care of you today." She shakes her head as I walk us over to the tiny table in my kitchen.

"You are taking care of me." I kiss her temple and sit her at the table. After grabbing the food and a couple of plates, I sit down and plate up stir-fry and spring rolls for the two of us before we dig into our meal. Caity looks around the apartment as she chews her food, taking in the single couch, one end table, and television on the wall with a furrowed brow.

"Did you just move in here?" she asks, crunching down on her cabbage spring roll.

"Uh, no." I put my fork down and run my hand through my hair. "I've lived here for almost four years now." This is it, this is when she realizes I'm nothing but a grown man-child that isn't worth her time.

She shrugs and bites into her food. "I like it. You have so much less crap to clean. I bet that's nice."

I sit back in my chair and huff a breath. "It doesn't bother you?"

"What?" She raises a brow.

"That I basically live like I'm one truckload away from skipping town?" I ask, waiting for her answer with baited breath.

Caity looks thoughtful for a moment as she ponders my question. "No, but that's because I know you aren't just going to skip town." She wipes her mouth on a napkin. "You've been here four years. If you were going to get bored and leave, you would have done it by now," she explains.

"I guess that's true." I got so used to moving around and never setting up shop, figuring I would never be around longer than a year, two at the most. I hadn't realized I had actually put down roots here. I may not have a house or a decorated apartment, but I have a stable job that I enjoy and a great group of friends. Apparently, all my worrying was for nothing.

She leans over and grabs my hand. "You don't need a lot of furniture or art on the walls to have a home. Home is more than just a place where you sleep, and it looks like you have one here in this town."

"I suppose I do." I squeeze her hand. "I guess I just never thought of it that way." She smiles and takes a few more bites of her food. Before I lose my nerve, I get up the courage to ask her about her own plans. "So, uh, since we've made so much progress on your house, have you decided whether or not you're going to sell it? Travel the world or whatever?"

Her eyes meet mine and she stares into them as she talks to me. "I actually got an offer in the mail today," she says, licking her lips before continuing. "They offered to pay cash for the house as is. I guess it's a nice neighborhood to raise a family in and the couple who contacted me have a pair of young kids." I swallow thickly. So, she's leaving then. All this has been for nothing. I start to nod and try to look happy for her, even as my heart is breaking in two. Now I know what it feels like. She eyes my face and leans in closer to me. "I turned them down, Noah," she says, her voice steady.

I swallow again, afraid to hope. "You did?"

"I did. I thought about it and I like the area, I've met some good people, and if it's such a great neighborhood, I'd probably like to raise my own family in that house. I do have some happy memories there." She looks up at me shyly and my body sags in relief.

"So, you're staying'?" I ask, needing to hear the words.

She nods and her smile widens. "I'm staying."

I whoop in delight and push my chair back before I pull her up and swing her around. She laughs in delight and I kiss her hard on the mouth. After a minute of kissing her soundly, I drop her to her feet. "Thank you, darlin'! That just made my whole damn day," I reveal.

"You're welcome," she says with a blush as she smiles up at me. "But I'm doing it for me. You being here is just a lovely bonus."

I return her smile, overjoyed at the news that our relationship no longer has a time clock on it. Out of the corner of my eye, I see the wedding invitation on my fridge and can't believe I almost forgot to ask. "Hey, uh, I was wondering if you would like to be my date for Amelia and Gabe's wedding? It's in two weeks and I'm sorry I forgot to ask sooner, but I'd really love it if you would come with me."

Her eyes narrow. "Were you holding out on me until you knew whether or not I was staying?"

I lift a shoulder. "Not consciously, no. I think I just assumed you would be my date and the whole asking part slipped my mind."

Okay." She bounces on her toes, totally unfazed by that. "I would have understood if you had. You would have been protecting yourself." She sits back at the table and finishes her food.

"I promise that wasn't my intent, but I'm glad you would have understood anyway." I finish up my last bite of food and take our dishes to the sink.

Caity wraps her arms around me from behind and presses her body close. "I know how you can make it up to me," she says. Her voice sounds extra sweet and I am immediately suspicious.

"You just said I didn't have anything to make up for," I declare knowing I'll say yes to anything she asks anyway.

"I know, and you don't, really. It's just that I saw your guitar case in the corner just now and was hoping I could finagle a song out of you," she admits quietly.

I dry my hands and turn around, grabbing her hand and marching her over to my couch where I sit her down. "If you want me to serenade you, darlin', all you have to do is ask. No finagling required."

She looks up at me with big eyes and a sweet smile. "Would you please sing to me, Noah? I love your voice and I've been watching the video of you from the talent show nonstop."

I feel the tips of my ears heat. "I'm not that

great," I say, a little abashed at the praise.

"Well, I think you're fantastic and I would love to hear you sing again, but not if it makes you uncomfortable." She's amazing and if I can sing in front of an auditorium full of people, I can certainly sing in front of her.

I grab my case and after taking the guitar out, I put it next to the couch. I strum a few chords to tune it and ask, "Any requests? I mostly know country songs."

"Whatever you want to play works for me," she says, making herself comfortable on the brown leather couch.

I think about all the songs I know, and come up with what I think is an appropriate tune for this woman. I start playing "My Best Friend," by Tim McGraw and watch her face as I sing her the lyrics about best friends who are also something more. Her eyes light up when I sing about no one ever making me feel the way she does and she blushes fiercely when I get to the lyrics about making love. I do my best to sing my heart out for her. Last time was about making amends, but this time is about where we are now and where I would like us to be. I have every hope that we'll get there and by the look of contentment on her face, I think she knows it too.

I lift my fingers off the guitar strings and look at her. Her eyes are heated as she stares at me, breathing a little harder than she was a moment ago. "You're going to want to put that guitar away now, Cowboy."

"Why's that, Caity-bug?" My eyes rake up and down her body, wanting to peel every layer of clothing off her to explore what's underneath.

"Because I am about to launch myself at you and I don't want it to get broken," she says, dead serious.

I chuckle and put my guitar back in its case. As soon as I turn around, Caity does indeed launch herself at me, but I'm able to quickly grab her and drape her over my lap as she grabs my shirt and pulls me down into a fiery kiss. She attacks my mouth in the best way, moving her lips over mine with passion and skill. Who knew my girl was such a little firecracker? Her hand slides into my hair and she runs her fingers through it before she tugs at it a little, making my scalp tingle. I run my tongue along the seam of her mouth and she opens for me. I dive in to taste her sweetness as I rub my hands along her sides, moaning along with each of her own whimpers and mews. As we continue to work each other up into a frenzy, she repositions herself so she's straddling me and starts grinding down on my erection. If we don't slow this down, things are going to progress a little too quickly and I promised myself and her we would go slow.

I break the kiss, panting out a breath. "Need to slow down, sweetheart."

She pouts. "Why?"

"This probably sounds dumb, but I want our first time to be special." Most of my experience with women has been about getting off and getting out the door, and I want more than that with Caity. I don't want to just have a quickie on the couch before we crash out for work in the morning. I want to romance this woman before I spend the night making love to her. I want to make her breakfast and make love to her again and again until we forget where I begin and she ends.

She licks her lips before rubbing them together. "It's not dumb, it's sweet, and I can wait." She tries to press her thighs together, but just ends up squeezing my legs, and while I don't want to go all the way tonight, I can still help her out.

"How about I give you a little something to tide you over, darlin'?" She nods furiously and I chuckle. "Okay, but clothes have to stay on." If our clothes come off I'm not sure I'll be able to keep my body in check. This woman drives me crazy.

She grumbles unhappily at my request. "Can you at least lose the shirt?" She runs her hands underneath my t-shirt and slides them up to my chest, rubbing them along the hair she finds there. "I've been dying to see you."

I can't say no to this woman. "All right." I grab the back of my shirt and peel it off. "But your top has to stay on."

She is staring at the planes of muscles on my torso and licks her lips. Her eyes meet mine. "Huh?" She shakes her head. "I mean, okay. I'll keep my top on." She leans back, grabs the hem of her blue sweater, and pulls it over her head revealing a pink, silky-looking camisole that shows off her perky breasts. If that wasn't bad enough, she puts her hands underneath and twists around until she slips a pink bra out from under the camisole.

"You fixin' to get spanked, Caity-bug?" I growl at my feisty little minx. She is temptation incarnate and every move she makes has my resolve weakening.

She smirks. "I'm still wearing a top," she sasses before leaning next to my ear. In a low, seductive tone, she whispers to me. "Let's save the spanking for next time. It's about time I took my cowboy for a ride." She nibbles on the lobe of my ear and starts grinding down on my lap.

"Goddamn," I grit out as she rubs herself all over me. What is this woman doing to me? I thought I would be the one blowing her mind with the physical stuff, but she's been a sweet, sultry surprise. I grab her ass and lift her up, only to slam her down harder and help her find that sweet spot that will have her seeing stars. She moans and keeps gyrating her hips, eventually leaning down to kiss me. Our mouths dance as our bodies move together, both building toward that inevitable climax. I try to think of ways to distract myself, but it's hard when I have this little firecracker going to town on my lap.

She breaks the kiss and leans back a little. "I'm close," she breathes out, moving faster. I reach up, pinch one of her nipples through her shirt with my fingers, and she explodes. "Ahhh," she cries and her face is a beautiful reflection of the ecstasy she's experiencing. She slows her movements, but I'm not done with her yet.

I flip her down onto the couch and bury myself between her legs, tilting my hips into her center until she starts building up again. "Noah … I…"

"Keep it going, sweetheart. I'm not letting you leave here until you can't form words," I vow as I keep thrusting my hips into her, peeling her tiny shirt up to her neck because I just can't help myself. Her skin is alabaster and smooth, with just a few of my favorite cinnamon-colored freckles sprinkled about. I kiss my way up to her breasts and take a nipple into my mouth, using my hand to tease and pinch the other one.

"I … thought … top … on…" she says between pants and moans.

I pop off her nipple. "It's still on. It's just relocated a little further north than before." I go back to my ministrations and thrust harder until I can tell she's close and I'm about to blow. I haven't come in my pants since I was a teenager, but I don't really care. All that matters to me now is getting her there before I go off. "C'mon, darling. You can do it."

After my words of encouragement and a few more thrusts, she flies apart again and I follow her over the edge, making a mess in my pants that I don't have the energy to care about. When I start to come down from the exquisite high, I still my movements and lean down to kiss her gently as she struggles to catch her breath. She looks up at me, dazed and thoroughly satisfied. Her mouth opens to speak, but the only sound that comes out is a contented moan that causes me to smirk. "There's that incoherence I was hoping for."

She slaps my shoulder but I can feel her laughing beneath me. I sit up and pull her top down before helping her to sit. Her hair is a mess and her glasses are askew, but she's never looked more beautiful. "That was nice."

I scoff. "That was a helluva lot more than nice, Caity-bug."

"It was amazing and mind-blowing and so, so good," she says. She leans over to kiss me gently as she catches her breath and comes down from our shared bliss. "But it was also nice." She pats my chest and stands up, a little wobbly on her feet. I give myself a mental high-five for that and go to stand up myself. My legs aren't fairing much better, and I unsteadily reach for my shirt and put it back on. She's got her hoodie back on and stuffs her bra in the front pocket.

"You don't have to leave, you know." I desperately need a change of pants, but I wouldn't mind cuddling for a bit.

"I know I don't, and I don't really want to," she tells me, grabbing her purse and heading for the door. "But you are just too darn sexy, Cowboy, so I'm going to take off before I ask you for another ride."

"I can respect that." I don't like it, but I respect it. It's me putting the brakes on after all.

I open the door for her and go to follow her out. She turns around and seems surprised to see me so close. "Where are you going?"

"I'm walking you to your car," I explain. She should know by now that I'm not letting her out of my sight if I don't have to.

She looks down at my jeans which are very

obviously a complete mess. "You sure about that?" she snickers.

"Oh, I reckon I can deal with the embarrassment if it means I know you're tucked away safely in your car." I'll walk around the whole damn complex with this stain on my jeans before I let her walk to her car alone.

"I don't think there's anything to be embarrassed about. A lot of older folks have problems with incontinence." She starts to walk away and I grab her hand and fall in step with her.

"I'm only twenty-eight, smartass," I say as we make our way to the parking lot.

"I know. A whole two years older than me. How will we deal with the age gap? Especially now that we need to be looking into adult diapers. It will be so confusing when we have our own kids."

My heart skips a beat and part of me thinks I should be afraid of her mention of us starting a family together so soon, but I'm not. In fact, the thought of a bunch of wild, red-haired little ones warms my heart. "I think we'll figure it out, Caity-bug." We get to her little hybrid and I open the door for her, leaning down to kiss her sweetly before she hops inside. "Buckle up now, darlin'." She dutifully buckles her seat belt and I shut the door, motioning for her to roll her window down and once it is, I rest my arms on the door. "Thanks for a wonderful evening, sweetheart. I had a good time."

She kisses my cheek. "Me too. See you tomorrow?"

"You know you will." I stand up and rap the top of the car with my knuckles and watch as she drives off, already missing her and wishing it was tomorrow already. I make my way back to my apartment and look around once I'm inside. Caity was right. I don't need furniture or art to make this a home, but I'm very certain I need her.

Chapter Nineteen
Caitlin

My muscles protest as I move from one pose to another, trying to follow along as best I can as Amelia guides both Madi and I in the movements. Amelia texted and invited me to join them for their weekly yoga in the park this Sunday morning. It didn't take much thought for me to respond in the affirmative. I said yes, not only because I wanted to spend time with them, but because I could use the stretching after all the work I finished up at home yesterday.

Noah had an away game on Friday and then Gabe's bachelor party last night, which he assured me consisted of video games and Mexican food, not that I didn't trust him anyway. He is spending the day today helping with wedding prep since he's the best man, so we haven't seen each other since Friday morning. I miss him and I needed a distraction, so I threw myself into ripping up the carpet and painting the master bedroom. I finally wanted to make it my own, and while I already had my own bed, I wanted to create an aesthetic that was more me and less my grandma.

Ripping up the carpet was easy enough and exposed gorgeous hardwood floors underneath. The once rose-colored walls are now a pale turquoise to offset the colorful quilts I had found in Gran's closet. I had them dry-cleaned and after painting yesterday morning, I arranged the room with my wrought-iron bed in the corner and I put them on top. They look great and go well with the older furniture I had already painted a pale yellow. I love how cozy it looks and I'm so glad I decided to keep the house. It just feels right, and if things with Noah keep going well, maybe he'll be moving in soon too.

"What has you so smiley over there?" Madi asks. "No one should be so happy at eight-thirty on a Sunday morning. I certainly am not," she grumbles as she holds her pose.

"I am," Amelia announces. "I am super, duper happy and excited." The woman practically exudes joy even as she tries to manipulate her pregnant body into looking like a twisted pretzel.

"You're getting married next weekend and your fiancé is doing most of the work. It makes sense that you'd be happy," Madi gripes.

"I did a lot of stuff too, I'll have you know. He just wants me to relax and not be stressed because of the baby." She rubs her belly and moves into another pose. I follow along clumsily, but manage to not lose my balance, so I'm counting it as a win. "Besides, there isn't much more to do. He checked up on the gardens yesterday and I think today is their final suit fitting. Once that's done he just needs to show up and look pretty."

Madi chuckles and I think she's moved on, but no such luck. "He'll look plenty pretty, but I still want to hear what has Caity looking so cheery," she says with a grin.

Amelia moves us into a sitting pose and my body rejoices at the break as I look over at the two women and try to formulate an answer to Madi's query. "I don't know. I guess I'm just really liking life here. I wasn't sure how I'd feel at a high school instead of a city library, but I like it. My house is turning into a place I could live for a long time, and I'm making some new friends," I say, gesturing to the two of them.

"Well, we are pretty darn amazing, but I think your smile has a little more to do with a certain football coach we all know," Madi ventures.

I smile involuntarily and Amelia squeals. "Ha-ha! Yes, it's totally because you and Noah are in love."

Love. I have thought about that word more than once over the last few weeks, and I'm sure I am in love with him. It would have been difficult not to fall in love with someone so caring and generous and funny. It certainly doesn't hurt that our physical chemistry is off the charts as well. I'm still thinking about our time on his couch as well as the heavy makeout session we had at my place Thursday night. My skin tingles and I flush at the memories, quickly trying to school my features before I speak.

"I do really like Noah and he is an amazing person. As far as love goes, well, if I am in love with him, I think he should be the first person to hear it," I tell them seriously. I don't want this to be something heard through the grapevine. He should hear it straight from me.

"Aw," Madi says. "You totally love him. This is so great. Now we can all be married and have babies together."

"Whoa," I hold up my hands. "No one said anything about marriage or babies."

"You don't want that?" Amelia asks, looking at me like I'm a crazy person if I say I don't.

"No. I mean yes, I absolutely do, but I don't know if Noah does. We haven't really talked about it and I wouldn't want to pressure him." I would love to marry Noah and have a family, but I also want to keep him forever and talking about that stuff so early could scare him.

Amelia taps her lips, thinking. "Hmm. I don't think he would feel pressured. He's a decisive guy. Honestly, he's probably already picked out a ring and everything," she says casually.

I pretend to plug my ears and hum. "Ah! Do not say that stuff. You'll jinx it."

Madi pulls my hands away from my face. "Nothing will jinx what you two have. I've seen you guys at school together and I have not seen him look at anybody or anything the way he looks at you. Not even the bacon cheeseburgers at The Goat."

"That's actually super high praise. He really loves those burgers," Amelia adds.

"Okay, but let's change the subject anyway. We're in a good place and I don't want to put any weird vibes out into the universe." I wave my hands in the air around me to clear away any bad luck. My feelings for teenage Noah felt deep but not anywhere near as rooted in my heart as they are now. Noah has been nothing but committed to our relationship, but I think there is still that small part of me that wonders if he'll ever love me as much as I love him.

"Fine, fine." Amelia moves us into the final pose and I relish the fact that I can now just lay here for five minutes.

"Do you have a dress for the wedding? I'm assuming you're coming because I want you there and you shouldn't anger a pregnant woman near her wedding day," Amelia mentions, only vaguely threatening harm should I answer the wrong way.

"I am coming, and I have a dress, but I kind of want to get something a little more formal. I don't know, what do you think?" I sit up and grab my phone, pulling up a photo of the plain, green dress I have had since college graduation. I haven't had many occasions to dress up, so I've just reused it time and time again.

Madi and Amelia look at my phone, then at each other, then at me. "We're going shopping," they say in unison.

"I know the perfect place," Amelia adds. She rolls up her yoga mat and I roll up the one she let me borrow. "I used to shop there all the time before I couldn't fit into non-maternity clothes."

"We'll hit up the stores after we grab some food," Madi announces as we walk over to Amelia's little red car. She was nice enough to pick us up this morning, saying she wanted to take advantage of her second trimester energy boost.

After dropping off our yoga mats, we walk a few blocks to a restaurant called Brekkie and order three breakfast burritos to go. Amelia explained that finding me a dress was way more important than sitting down for a meal. I disagree, but I'm also the one who needs their help to pick out an appropriate outfit, so I'll go along with it. Once we're back in Amelia's car, we dig into our food and she points us toward the downtown area of the city. We talk about my style preferences and after I explain that I prefer comfort over style, Amelia and Madi look at each other. Amelia looks back at me in the rearview mirror. "It's a good thing we got the burritos to-go, because I think we're going to have to go all out today."

I have a moment of panic at what that means for my body and my wallet, but I relax when she pulls into the parking lot of a vintage consignment store. At least my bank account won't take an enormous hit. Now that I'm not selling the house, I'll need to be more mindful of my budget.

The three of us exit the vehicle and I stop in front of the window. On display is a red, velvet, vintage cocktail dress. It's strapless and has a full skirt. It's straight out of the 1950s and I love it. It looks like it's in amazing shape too.

"Should we go in and you can try it on?" Amelia asks, smiling at my obvious desire to own the dress.

I nod excitedly and the two women drag me inside. I luck out that the dress is in my size and I head back to a dressing room to try it on. Once I have it zipped up, I step out and look at myself in the mirror. The dress is so comfortable and I look great in it. I spin around and see Amelia smiling at me and Madi starts a slow clap. "So, it looks okay?"

"Okay? You look scorching hot and I will be surprised if Noah doesn't have a heart attack on sight," Amelia comments.

"I'd me more surprised if he didn't jump your bones," Madi remarks.

I blush at the thought and I get an idea. The dress is for a special occasion, and maybe that night can be special in another way too. I bite my lip as I consider the possibilities. "Well, I'm definitely taking the dress, but I still need some shoes." Amelia starts to speak, but I hold up my hand. "I draw the line at used shoes. But, um, do you think you guys could tell me where I could find some new clothes to wear under the dress?" I dip my head and can feel the heat in my cheeks.

"Like a new bra?" Madi asks.

"Uh, kind of." I hesitate spelling it out. Maybe this isn't the kind of thing girlfriends talk about. If not, movies have grossly misinformed me.

Amelia snaps her fingers. "Oh, you mean lingerie," she says with a bob of her blonde head.

My face reddens and I move back into the dressing room. "Um, yeah, that." I take off the dress and change back into the comfy clothes I dressed in for yoga before pulling open the curtain to see both of them giggling. "What?"

Madi shakes her head. "You're so cute, getting

embarrassed about lingerie." She weaves her hand through my arm and steers me toward the checkout. "Well, don't be. Amelia and I talk about all sorts of crazy, personal stuff and it's no big deal."

"Really?" I ask, happy and a little afraid of what kind of information they may try to pull from me in the future.

"Yeah, totally," Amelia says as we get to the cashier. "Except Madi isn't allowed to tell me about her sex life anymore since she's married to my brother. " She makes a mock-gagging gesture and I chuckle.

"But now I have you to talk to about all the amazing stuff I get to try with Owen. There's this one thing he docs with his tongue..." she starts.

"Oh, God. Please, stop." Amelia fake-gags again and walks toward the exit.

Madi cackles and I laugh under my breath. After purchasing the dress, we go back outside and see Amelia leaning against her car. "All right, you two troublemakers, get in," she says, pointing to the passenger doors.

We laugh and hop in the car. I'm so happy to finally have a couple of girlfriends to hang out with. I thought I was happy with my life in the city, but I think I was just going through the motions. Since moving here, I've crawled out of my shell a bit and have some good relationships going. I've come a long way from high school, even if I still spend all my time in a library or with Noah. I'm different now, more confident, and I'm going to use some of that newfound confidence with my boyfriend this weekend. He wants our first time to be special. Well, I'm going to help make it as special as it can get.

Chapter Twenty
Noah

The music starts and I watch as Madi and Owen make their way down the aisle. I'm already up front with Gabe, standing beside him as his best man. I pat my front left pocket for the hundredth time, making sure the rings are still safely tucked away. I have one job tonight and I'm not going to screw it up. Owen drops Madi off to the side and steps next to me. "Two down, one to go," he whispers. "You're next, big guy."

I chuckle and nudge him with my elbow. "Let's make it through this wedding before you start planning mine, huh?"

"Fine, fine." The music changes to some classical song and we all straighten up. Gabe looks anxious, but not in a bad way, more like he can't stand still until he sees his bride. When she finally emerges on the arm of her father, his eyes widen and I swear he looks like he might tear up. Amelia is dressed in a pale-blue gown that accentuates her growing belly. Her hair is in a series of intricate-looking braids with some pieces falling out here and there. She looks ethereal, like some kind of fairy princess. A look made all the more real by the fact we are in the gardens of one of the city's fanciest hotels. As beautiful as she looks, she doesn't hold a candle to my girl.

I almost fell to my knees when Caity opened the door for me earlier. She was wearing a classic, red cocktail dress that had some of the softest fabric I ever put my hands on. And you can believe getting my hands on her in that dress was one of the first things I did, claiming her mouth for a good five minutes until she pushed me off, complaining about messed-up hair and wrinkled suits. She changed her tune when we arrived here later, though, kissing me soundly before fixing her loose curls and reapplying lipstick in the mirror of my truck before hopping out like she hadn't just set my world on fire. Caity has lit up my life brighter than the sun on a hot summer day and not just with her kisses, but with all the affection and care she shows me.

Amelia finally makes it up to the front and kisses her dad on the cheek before taking Gabe's offered hand and stepping up beside him. The officiant starts the ceremony and I listen to her talk about love, commitment, and partnership. As I process everything she's saying, I keep my eyes on Caity, she watches the ceremony with a small smile on her face and when she catches me watching her, she winks at me and I'm gone. I have fallen so deeply in love with this woman and I don't want to wait any longer before telling her. We already lost out on more than ten years because I was a scared jackass, and I'm not willing to lose any more time. I told Owen to hold off on planning my wedding, but I'm right there too, already thinking about how soon I can propose and tie my Caity-bug to me completely.

I'm staring at my girl so intently, daydreaming about the future, that I miss my cue. Gabe taps my shoulder and I reluctantly turn to him. "Yeah?" I ask dumbly.

He give me a sardonic look. "Rings?"

"Oh, right." I chuckle and reach into my pocket to pull out the ring box before placing the two rings in his palm.

He clasps my shoulders. "Thanks."

I nod and watch as he and Amelia exchange their own vows, promising to love and cherish one another as they slip the rings over the other's left finger. The officiant proclaims them husband and wife and announces them to the small crowd of family and friends who have gathered to celebrate. Gabe leans in and they kiss, not entirely appropriately, but hey, we're not in a church. Then they walk hand in hand back down the aisle to the tent that has been set up for the reception. Madi and Owen follow and I bring up the rear, stopping by the second row to grab my girl.

I offer my arm when she stands next to me. "Shall we?" I ask, a wide smile on my face every time I'm near her.

She smiles brightly, takes my arm, and I lead the two of us into the reception. "That was a beautiful wedding. Of course, I haven't ever been to one, but still. Everyone looks so nice and the gardens are gorgeous. It's like a fairy tale," she says wistfully.

I steer us to our assigned table. We're sitting with Owen, Madi, Mike Lassiter, Amelia's department chair, and his husband Lee. I pull the chair out for Caity and take my seat next to her, scooting our chairs closer together so I can put my arm around the back. "Is that what you would want for your wedding, Caity-bug? A fairy tale?"

She looks at me with a furrowed brow. "I never really thought about it, actually. I mean, I had daydreams of a future with a husband and kids, but it was always just a fantasy. I had never gotten close to anything like that before, so I suppose I didn't really let myself get too caught up in it. I didn't want to get my hopes up." She shrugs like it's no big deal that she never allowed herself to dream of a future with anyone.

I think more about her words and I lean in a little, lowering my voice for just her. "You said you hadn't gotten close to anything like that before. Does that mean you feel like you're close to something like that now?"

She blushes and opens her mouth to answer, but we're interrupted by the announcement that it's our table's turn at the buffet line. She scoots her chair back and I hop up to go with her, placing my hand on the small of her back as we make our way to the food. "We aren't finished with this conversation, darlin'. Just so you're aware," I inform her.

Her pearly teeth bite down on her lip for a moment, but her eyes are bright with mirth and not nerves. "I know," she tells me and grabs my hand. "I want to finish it too, but maybe not at a table with four other people."

"Fair enough," I say and grab a plate for her before taking my own. We pile our plates high with all the delicious-looking Mexican food.

I get to the end of the line and see a serving tray covered with Yorkshire puddings. "What are those, muffins?" Caity asks and I bark a laugh.

"Those are Yorkshire puddings, or the one compromise Amelia gave to her father as far as the food was concerned." I grab one and spoon some of the accompanying gravy on top. "Better take one if you don't want to offend Arthur." She grabs one but foregoes the gravy.

We find our way back the table and chat with everyone while we eat and talk about the wedding. I introduce Caity to Mike and his husband, and she and Lee seem to hit it off over their mutual appreciation for *The Lord of the Rings*. They continue to chat with one another, and I enjoy seeing Caity come out of her shell even more. I'm so proud of her. She's not really shy and awkward, she's just a little reserved in new situations. Once she's comfortable, she really shines and I absolutely enjoy watching it happen. I also love how seamlessly she fits into my life here. She's the missing puzzle piece I've been waiting on and I'm so happy the wait is finally over.

We finish our food just as Amelia and Gabe step onto the wooden dance floor for their first dance. Taylor Swift's "Lover" starts to play and they sway to the music, lost in each other as the rest of us stand by and hope for a love as sweet as theirs. After a minute, the DJ calls everyone else up to join them and I stand before holding my hand out to Caity. "Dance with me, Caity-bug?"

She nods, but after she's placed her warm hand in mine, she tells me, "I haven't danced that often, so don't expect much."

"Darlin', you could be a prima ballerina or have two left feet and I wouldn't notice. The only thing I care about right now is that I get to hold you in my arms." Her cheeks tinge pink and I lead us to a spot with plenty of room just in case, spinning her around before I pull her into my body. I grab one of her hands and slide it over my shoulder before I take the other and place it on my chest, circling my hands to grasp her lower back. She leans into me and I inhale the berry scent wafting off her hair as we glide from side to side, and I enjoy the feel of her body next to mine. I want this dance to last forever, I want her to be mine forever, and I think it's about time I told her that. The song switches over to bouncier tune, so I steer us to the side of the dance floor. "Do you think we could finish that conversation now, darlin'?"

Caity bobs her head and I grab her hand and lead her back out to the gardens where the ceremony was held. I stride over to a bench that sits beneath a wooden archway lined with flowers and vines. We sit and I see Caity shiver slightly. The early October evening has grown a little chilly, so I take off my suit jacket and drape it over her shoulders, scooting next to her and grabbing her hands. "So, earlier we were talking about whether you felt like you were close to something real. Something permanent. Before you answer that, I want to give you something," I say. I reach into my suit and pull out the envelope with her name on it that's been burning a hole in my pocket all evening. It's not much, and I'm not as good with words as she is, but I wanted to do this for her. "A long time ago you took a chance on me without knowing whether it would work out. I want to do the same for you."

"Noah, you don't have to..." I cut her off with a finger pressed to her lips.

"Please, just read it, Caity-bug," I ask, begging her with my eyes to play along for me.

She opens the envelope, pulls out the letter, and I watch her read: *I love you, Caitlin Walsh.*

Beneath it was written: *Do you love me? Check one.*

Two boxes labeled "yes" and "no" were underneath. Her emerald eyes shine with moisture when she looks up at me and laughs. "I don't have a pen."

I tuck a rogue curl behind her ear and smile softly at her. "You could just tell me, you know." I stroke her cheek with the backs of my fingers and her eyes drift shut. "Look at me, Caity-bug." She does and I take a deep breath. "I love you, sweetheart. I loved you back then and was too stupid to admit it to myself and everyone else, too caught up in my own insecurities to put us first and tell you. I love you still and I'm not so stupid anymore, and I wanted to let you know. You are the most warm-hearted, loving, and beautiful person I know. You've always believed in and encouraged me and continue to do it. I love you so much, Caity-bug. I know we haven't always been on the same page, and if you don't love me yet, I'll understand and wait until you do, even if that takes another eleven years." I lean in and touch our foreheads together. I want to kiss her, but I need to know how she feels too.

She reaches up and lightly grasps my neck with both hands. When she sniffles, I glance over and see that a few tears have escaped, so I brush them aside with my thumbs. She takes a breath and her eyes shine with love and happiness when they meet mine. "I love you too, Noah. So, so much. There was never a time when I didn't love you. I was just a little mad about it for a while."

I huff a small laugh before pulling her into me for a sweet kiss on the lips. "You can be mad about it for as long as you like, darlin', just as long as you still love me at the end of the day."

She laughs and uses her hold on my neck to pull my lips down to hers once more. This time the kiss starts sweet, but quickly turns hungry as we alternate taking each other's tongues into our mouths. Her hands move to my chest and she grips my shirt like her life depends on it. My hands slip under my jacket to skate across the bare skin of her shoulders and she whimpers before breaking us apart, her breath coming in spurts as her hands still cling to my shirt. "How long do you have to stay?"

I see the heat in her gaze and there is no mistaking where she wants us to be instead. I look down at the watch on my wrist. "Um, my speech is, uh…" She chuckles and I glare at her. "Hey, don't laugh. It's your fault all the blood isn't exactly in my brain right now."

She lifts a shoulder. "Sorry, not sorry?"

I laugh and finally have access to my brain cells. "My speech is after they cut the cake, so another forty minutes I think." I wish I could leave and be with her right now, but it's also the wedding of my close friends and I don't want to bail, even if they would both understand why.

She twists her lips. "I can wait forty minutes.

Especially if there is cake to hold me over. And I saw a table filled with cookies and churros, so that will distract me for a bit too," she says with a smile.

I stand and adjust myself, not bothering to hide just how badly she's affected me. "Well, I'm glad one of us will be distracted. I have to try and speak coherently in front of everybody when I clearly want to be doing something very different."

She stands up and pats my chest. "You'll be great. You're the most personable man I have ever met. Everybody loves you." She leans up and kisses my cheek. "That includes me."

And with that knowledge, I'm no longer nervous about my best man speech. I have the love of a good woman and I can see a bright future for the two of us. I'm on top of the world.

Chapter Twenty-One
Caitlin

The living room is dark when we step into my house. I flick on the light switch as I shut the door and lock it after Noah steps through. His jacket has been covering my shoulders since we had our talk outside in the gardens, and I shrug it off, folding it and draping it over the back of the couch. I was hoping the evening would end with us here, but now that it has, my nerves are getting the best of me. My fingers run over the smooth material of the jacket a few times, and I feel Noah's warm presence as he steps behind me. His hands rest on top of my shoulders as he leans down next to me. "We don't have to do anything you don't want to do, Caity-bug. I'm happy just being around you," he says, his voice low and full of patience and understanding.

My head hits his shoulder as I lean back against him. "Thank you. I do want to do things. I'm just a little nervous is all," I breathe out.

Noah kisses my cheek and spins me around. "If it helps, I'm nervous too. We can take things slow and see what happens if that feels good to you." His hazel eyes are shining down at me and I fall even more in love with him for how wonderful he's being right now.

I nod and rub my lips together. "Okay." I think about what I set up earlier that day and back away from him holding up three fingers. "Give me three minutes before you come into the bedroom, okay?" His head bobs, a small smile on his face, and I spin around to dash down the hallway.

I hustle into the room and pull back the sheets on the bed. Before Noah picked me up, I set a bunch of LED candles out around the room, so I take a minute to go over to each one, turning them on to create a lovely glow. I wanted it to look romantic, but I also didn't want to have to think about the house burning down while we were making love. I stop short at the thought and smile. I love Noah Hunter and he loves me. Even if we're both a little nervous about tonight, the fact that we love each other makes everything seem less scary.

Going to my closet next, I shuck off my dress, making sure to hang it up with care. It's old velvet and I want to wear it again. I head over to the bathroom for a quick appearance check, hitting the light and giving myself a once over. I have a certain glow about me, and I know it's the love I'm feeling for Noah shining through every pore in my body. I pull the hair comb off the right side of my head and fluff my curls a little, taking a look at the lingerie I purchased and hoping I made the right call. I'm wearing a white, sheer lace corset that buttons down the front and some lacy white boy shorts. There is very little left to the imagination, but I liked the way it looked in the store and I know deep down that no matter what I'm wearing, Noah will love it.

After I'm fully dressed, or mostly undressed, I climb onto the bed and try to twist my body into a couple of different poses, but I start to feel foolish, so I end up just sitting on my knees at the edge of the bed, trying not to tug at the hem of my corset while I wait for him. After another minute, there's a knock at the door and the butterflies start up in my stomach. "Come in," I manage to say and not squeak.

Noah slowly opens the door and looks around the room at the candles. He takes everything in and smiles when his eyes land on the vase of paper roses on my nightstand. I brought them home to keep in my room so I could look at them every night before I go to bed, thinking it will help me dream of him if I do, but it turns out he's on my mind all the time regardless of whether I have a physical reminder. Noah's love and attention is all I need, and right now I'm about to get it in spades. His eyes move across the bed and when they land on me, they widen and fill with heat. He licks his lips and I feel maybe I picked the right outfit after all. He steps into the room, having already removed his socks, shoes, and tie. The first two buttons of his shirt are undone, teasing me with just the tiniest hint of flesh. He still has the black belt securing his slacks in place and I like that he kept the barrier of his own clothes on in case I changed my mind. I won't.

Noah gets next to the bed and holds his hand out to me. When I slip my hand inside, he pulls me to my feet. While I stand in front of him, he holds both my arms wide and takes a step back. "I wanted to see all of you. So beautiful," he tells me earnestly, his eyes raking up and down my body. I tremble, but it isn't from the temperature of the room. If anything, I feel like I could spontaneously combust I'm so hot inside, but I'm shivering because of how his gaze is making me feel. I feel stunning, cherished, and above all, so very loved.

He continues to look at me, and I finally get some courage and move closer to him. He drops my arms and I move to grab his with my hands. "Now that you've seen me, what are you going to do with me?" I tease.

A low, growling noise rumbles from his chest and he grabs my hips, pulls me close, and slashes his mouth down to mine. The kiss is hard and desperate like a hungry man who has just been given an all-you-can-eat pass at the buffet. His tongue demands entrance into my mouth and I happily give into it, opening for him on a whimper so we can devour each other. His hands roam my body and land on my behind where he grabs both cheeks in his big hands and gives them a firm squeeze as he grinds his erection into my belly. I gasp and he takes the opportunity to dive deeper into my mouth, owning me and claiming my soul as his own. He can have it because it's always belonged to him anyway.

Noah breaks the kiss and spins me around before pulling my back to his front, holding me in place with his hands on my soft stomach. He leans down and kisses the spot where my shoulder meets my neck, a place I had no idea was so sensitive and erotic until this very moment. I take the opposite arm and run my hand into his hair, enjoying the feel of the soft locks as they glide through my fingers. While my hand tangles in his hair, his hands run up to my breasts and gently massage each one. I have never been particularly happy with my smaller chest, but they are clearly more than enough to please Noah. He continues to squeeze lightly, and I moan and gasp when he pinches my nipples through the sheer fabric. I'm already so turned on I feel I'm going to die if he doesn't get inside me, but Noah doesn't seem in a hurry, so I try to hold myself off and enjoy every second we're together. He pops off my shoulder and tilts my head back to claim my mouth once more. We kiss and his hands stop kneading my body. My mind tries to locate them and when I feel cool air hit my chest, I realize he's unbuttoning the corset. It took me forever to get it done up and he's undoing it in seconds without even looking at it. Not fair.

Once the corset is unbuttoned, he takes it and tosses it behind us to parts unknown. One of his hands slides beneath the waist of my panties, and I gasp when he starts rubbing my clit, the other hand moving back up to cup my breast. I'm already so worked up and he has very skilled fingers, so it doesn't take me long to get close. My breathing quickens as he continues to slide his fingers through my folds and rub the spot that winds me up. I'm panting and my head hits his shoulder. "I'm … so close," I pant out, pushing my center into his hand to create even more delicious friction.

"That's right, darlin'. Just let go. I've got you," he purrs into my ear, rubbing me quicker now. When his other hand pinches my nipple, my whole body tightens up before I explode. There are fireworks behind my eyes and I cry out his name, feeling like my body just exploded into a thousand points of light. He continues to rub and I go impossibly higher, keening sounds I've never made before coming out of my mouth. I didn't think I could come this hard, but here we are. Noah brings me down gently, slowing his movements before stopping entirely, taking his hand out from my panties and licking his fingers. "Mmm, just like strawberries."

His words barely register as I'm still trying to catch my breath and my legs shake with the effort to keep myself upright. Noah sees this and scoops me up into his arms before laying me down on the bed. Now that I'm horizontal, I take time to catch my breath and come back to my body. When I feel slightly more grounded, I look over to Noah as he stands at the foot of the bed with a grin on his face, and when I see that he is still fully clothed, I frown, pointing at the offending articles. "You need to lose those," I order between breaths.

He chuckles and starts unbuttoning his shirt. "You don't want to do it for me, darlin'?

I shake my head slightly. "I'm still trying to recover from those intense orgasms, so you'll have to do it yourself. It's your own fault, really."

He shrugs a shoulder, looking very smug. "Sorry, not sorry?" he echoes my earlier sentiment. I laugh until he finally finishes with the buttons and loses the shirt and the one underneath. Now I have the most amazing view of the golden skin and dark-brown hair that covers his deliciously chiseled chest. His arms are another sight to behold, all lean muscle and strength. The clink of his belt buckle hits my ears quickly followed by the unzipping of his pants. Once those are off, he's in nothing but his black boxer briefs which are tented quite dramatically in the front.

I point at his erection. "Seems like we should do something about that."

He raises a brow before pushing the briefs down to his ankles. When he pops back up I get my first look at him and he is glorious. "You think so, huh?"

I am speechless, too busy taking in the sight of his very erect penis. I nod my head and babble the words, "Uh-huh."

He chuckles and I feel the bed dip as he sits next to me. "May I?" he asks, hooking his fingers into the sides of my panties. I lift my hips and he slips them off before tossing them on the pile of clothes. He lays next to me, propping his head on his elbow and taking his other hand to brush the hair away from my face. "You want to keep going, Caity-bug?"

I look up at his face and see love, affection, and just the slightest bit of vulnerability. He's putting himself out there again and leaving the final call up to me. I reach down and grab him, slowly moving my hand up and down as I tease his arousal. He groans and I smile at the low, gravelly sound. "Does this answer your question?"

He kisses my lips lightly and pulls back. "It does, but I still want to hear the words, darling. I need to hear that you want this. Want me," he admits.

My smile gets impossibly wider. "I love you, Noah. I want you to make love to me." I continue to pull and tug him as his breathing quickens. "I'm on the shot and I'm clean, but we can use something if you want."

"I'm clean too, and I'm good with nothing between us if you are." He reaches down and removes my hand. "I'm going to need you to stop that, though, because I want this to last and that feels too good," he tells me, his eyes stern.

I pout. "Fine. I guess I'll just have to do something else with my hands." I bring them up to my chest and start playing with my own breasts, tugging and pulling on them until I'm worked up all over again.

Noah bats my hands away while crawling between my legs. "Oh, no, you don't." He lines himself up with my center and looks into my eyes. "You want something to do with your hands, why don't you reach up and hold on tight while I make you mine?" I obey and move my hands to his back, holding on tight as he starts to slide into me.

The stretch feels amazing and I tell him so. "Yes, that feels so good, Noah. I want more," I tell him, wanting to feel each inch of him as soon as possible.

"What's the magic word?" he grits out. He's going gently but I can tell he doesn't want to hold back anymore and I don't want him to.

"Harder," I breathe out.

He huffs and looks into my eyes. "Are you sure? I don't want to hurt you, Caity-bug?"

I move my hands down to his rear and grab both sides, pulling him further into me. "And if I want it to hurt a little?" I smile coyly and bring my hips up to take in even more.

"Goddamn. You're goin' to be the death of me, woman," he says, looking like he's experiencing pain and pleasure at the same time.

I keep moving my hips until he's almost completely inside. "Yeah, but what a way to go." The last thread of his control finally snaps and he slams the rest of the way in. I gasp and cry out, "Yes."

He pulls out a little before thrusting back inside. He hits hard and deep until moans are spilling from my mouth without my knowledge or permission. He does it again, this time with a grunt and a few swear words are said by both of us. "You feel amazing," he tells me as he continues to thrust in and out, our hips moving together and the friction between our bodies providing a nice warmth.

I try to reciprocate the sentiment, but I can't form coherent thoughts at the moment, so I simply reach up and kiss him. Trying to tell him with my body what I can't with words right now. I love you. This is the best it's ever felt in my entire life. You know just what I want and need. Can we spend the rest of our lives doing this and only this? He picks up speed and reaches an arm under my back to lift my hips, and the new angle feels even better. I dig my heels into the bed for leverage as he pounds into me. "Almost ... almost..." I trail off just before another orgasm comes over me, this one even more intense than the last two. I'm pretty sure I find myself on another plane of existence for a moment before I hear Noah grunt, crying my name out as he swells and topples over the edge with me.

Our movements slow and we kiss as much as two people who are completely out of breath can. I run my hands up and down his back lightly and he shivers which creates a fun sensation in my own body. Finally, he pulls out and collapses next to me, pulling me over so that my head is resting on his chest. It's covered with a sheen of sweat, but I don't mind since I'm in the same boat. I run my fingers through the small layer of chest hair, enjoying the small tickle it causes on my skin and look up at him. "That was pretty freakin' awesome, Cowboy."

His chest rumbles as he laughs and he tilts his

head down to kiss the top of mine. "It certainly was, Caity-bug." He brushes his fingers through the tangles of my hair. "Thank you," he says.

"For what?" I ask, enjoying the feeling of his solid body under mine.

"For not giving up on me. For giving us another chance. For loving me." He kisses the top of my head again. "For everything. I love you, Caity."

I prop my chin up on his chest and look him in the eyes. "I love you too, Noah." I reach up and sweep my lips across his in a sweet kiss. "And you don't have to thank me. Loving you is the easiest thing in the world," I tell him, feeling a peace I haven't felt in my entire life. I lay my head back onto his chest and let the steady rhythm of his heart guide me into the best sleep I've had in years.

Chapter Twenty-Two
Noah

Random noises wake me from what must have been the best night's sleep I've ever had, even though there was little actual sleeping involved. After making love the first time, Caity and I slept for a bit, but I woke her up once before midnight to take her from behind while we lay next to each other and she woke me up earlier this morning to ride me after she secured my hands to her bedframe with my tie. I knew my girl was a spitfire, but I had no idea just how much until she started lacing my wrists together. I've never been more turned on in my life than when she was on top of me. She calls me Cowboy, but she's the one who rides like she grew up in the saddle. I harden at the memories and turn on my side, expecting to see Caity sleeping soundly next to me, but the bed is empty and that's when I hear the noises again. It sounds like they're coming from the kitchen, so I hop out of bed to find my briefs.

I glance over at the clock and see that it's almost eleven in the morning. I guess we slept a little harder than I thought. Well, we earned it, and I'm excited that it's Fall Break. It means I get a whole week with just me and Caity, making love all day and night and sleeping if off just to do it all over again. I finally locate my underwear and slip them on, still hard thinking about all the things I want to do with my little spitfire. I wander down the hall and enter the kitchen, stopping when I see Caity reaching up into the pantry for a cereal box. She's wearing one of her old, baggy t-shirts, but since she's reaching up on her tippy toes, I can see she isn't wearing any panties. I get a peek of her round behind and a low growl makes its way out of me. She spins around and clutches the box of sugary cereal to her chest. "You scared me!" She puts the box on the counter and turns toward the cabinets where she grabs a couple of bowls. Her back is to me, so she doesn't see me walking toward her. "I don't have a lot of food in the house and I know it's basically lunchtime, but I figured we could have a small bowl of cereal and then maybe go out," she says matter-of-factly.

I make my way behind her and grab her hips. "I don't want cereal," I say with authority.

She looks at me over her shoulder. "Okay. I think I have some toast or something." I shake my head and she frowns. "Aren't you hungry?"

"Starving," I tell her right before I pull her hips back, drop to my knees, and push her shirt up.

"Noah, what are you … uuuhh." Her words trail off into a moan as I start to lick her from behind. She starts to move her hips against me and I get better access to her wet core. I lick from her center up to her clit, sliding my tongue through her folds and dipping my tongue into her every now and then, tasting the sweet honey I know now is just for me. I hear her hand slap the counter and the other comes back and grabs onto my hair. She pulls it a little, but the sting feels good and keeps me grounded enough that I don't go off in my briefs. I dip my tongue in and out while I move my fingers up to her clit and start to rub. When she gets even wetter, I know she's close, so I keep licking and rubbing before I move my mouth up to her hard nub and suck as hard as I can. She goes off like the little firecracker she is and I keep going, eating her throughout her orgasm.

She starts to come down and I lean back on my heels before standing up, wiping my face with the back of my hand. She turns around and before she can talk, I close my mouth over hers and work my tongue inside, just like I did with her core. She moans and grips my forearms as they hold onto her hips, my fingers digging in hard enough to leave a bruise as I lift her up onto the counter and step between her legs. She opens them for me and reaches down to pull me out of my briefs. Once I'm freed, she wiggles to the edge and I slam into her in one movement. She breaks the kiss to cry out and I pull back, looking into her eyes to see if I've hurt her. There's nothing but heat and passion there, and she pulls me back into her for a kiss, moving her legs to my back, digging her feet into my ass. I groan and thrust into her, grabbing onto the counter with one hand for leverage, grabbing her hip with the other to hold her steady as I pound into her over and over again.

It's quick and dirty, but it feels so good. Her warm center grips me tight as I slide in and out. I take my hand off the counter and grab her leg, hooking it over the inside of my elbow to change the angle. Her lips fall away from mine and we both pant out our breaths. She reaches between us to rub her clit with her fingers and after a couple of seconds she comes, hard. Her free hand digs into my back and I'll be surprised if I'm not covered in half-moon shapes from how much her nails are piercing my skin. I don't mind, though. I will proudly wear this woman's marks all over me. I keep grinding into her and she moans. "Give me one more, darlin'. You can do it," I say, wanting to take her higher than she ever thought possible.

Caity shakes her head and I pull her shirt collar to the side, taking my mouth down to lick and nibble at the spot on her shoulder that drove her wild last night. I thrust harder, making sure my pelvis is hitting her just right as I bite down on her shoulder. When she cries out one last time I thank my lucky stars because I was so close. Now, I can let go, following her over the edge of pleasure. Trying to hold off was tough, but it was worth it to feel how hard her insides are squeezing me, holding onto me like this is where I belong, and I do. I belong inside this woman, beside this woman, with her wherever she goes and supporting her through the good and the bad. I'm going to marry this woman as soon as she'll let me.

My thrusting slows to a stop and I kiss the spot I just bit. I didn't break the skin, but she'll have a little mark of her own too. She's still catching her breath, so I kiss the tip of her nose, her cheeks, and her forehead before I put my finger underneath her chin and tilt her head up to me. "You doing okay, Caity-bug?"

Her head bobs lightly and she has a lazy smile on her face, her green eyes looking slightly dazed. I brush my lips lightly against hers and pull out. I tuck myself back into my briefs and grab a clean washcloth. I run it under warm water at the sink before returning to her and cleaning up the mess I made. She reaches for the cloth. "I can do that."

I simply grunt and continue my cleaning. When I'm done, I walk it over to the laundry room and toss it in the washer. I get back and help her down from the counter, pulling her into a hug and resting my chin on top of her head. "I like taking care of you, darlin."

She hums contentedly. "I like it too." She hugs me tightly before stepping back. "But we probably shouldn't eat in this kitchen until we clean it up too."

I chuckle and go to grab the cleaning supplies from under the sink. We spend a few minutes cleaning the counters and when we're satisfied that all is sanitary, we put everything away. Caity taps her finger on her chin. "You know, we cleaned me up, and we cleaned up the kitchen, but nobody has cleaned you up."

I smirk. "You are correct. And what would you

like to do about that?"

"Well," she says as she grabs my hand and starts pulling me out of the kitchen. "How about we hop in the shower, I clean you up, and then we go get some lunch?" A wicked smile plays on her face, and I think she just came up with the best idea ever.

"Well, I'd say that sounds like a mighty fine idea, sweetheart. I do have one condition, though," I say, trying to keep my face serious.

She stops walking and turns around. "And what is that?"

I grab her hips and bring her back to feel that I'm already getting hard again. "My condition is that you dirty me up a bit more before cleaning me."

She reaches around and squeezes my ass before standing on her toes to give me a deep, passionate kiss. "I think I can manage that." She grabs my hand and steers me back to the bedroom and into the shower, where we spend the next few hours getting dirty over and over again.

****

We don't quite make it to The Greedy Goat in time for lunch and instead arrive for more of an early dinner. It's no bother really because it meant that Caity and I christened her shower and then she took me in her mouth twenty minutes later before I took her from behind while she put some scratch marks in the paint on top of her dresser. It took us a while to find the motivation to leave the house, but with promises of good food and more orgasms later, I was able to coax her into my truck. Luckily, I keep a change of clothes in my gym bag that's always stowed in my truck, so I don't need to hang out in my suit from yesterday.

I open the large, wooden door to the pub and escort Caity inside, putting my hand at the small of her back, not wanting to break my connection from her even for a moment. We head over to a small table in a more secluded corner so that I can keep her all to myself. I stop to pull her chair out, but she reaches up to kiss my cheek before stepping back. "I'm going to the restroom before we sit," she tells me.

Caity turns to go, but I grab her hand to stop her before pulling her body back into mine. "Don't be gone long or I'll be forced to come in after you," I profess. I'm completely serious too. I don't want to be away from my Caity-bug any longer than necessary.

"Don't threaten me with a good time." She winks and I reluctantly let go of her hand so she can go to the ladies' room. I sit down and grab a menu, perusing the food selections that I am already very familiar with. I'm going to need a lot of protein and carbohydrates to replenish all my spent energy and ensure I have more for later. I smirk, thinking of all the things Caity and I can try since we have a whole week off from work to explore one another.

The sound of footsteps approach and I look up with a grin, only for it to promptly fall off my face. It's Tiffani the server, and she's got that look in her eye again. The one that says she's ready to get her flirt on no matter how much the other person doesn't reciprocate. I didn't want her attentions before and I certainly don't want them now that I'm taken. I brace myself for an awkward encounter and she doesn't disappoint.

"Hey there, handsome. It's about time you showed up here." She comes right up next to me and the cloying smell of her perfume hits my nose, stinging my eyes. "I was starting to wonder if you'd forgotten all about me." Her phony pout is irritating. I had forgotten all about her up until this very moment, but as much as I dislike this woman hitting on me, I don't want to be rude. I thought I had made myself clear many times before, but I guess she'll need one more reminder.

"Listen, Tiffani," I say as she runs her hand down my arm. I promptly remove it with my own and harden my voice. "I appreciate that you work hard and like to flirt with the customers, but I'm not the guy to be doing that with. I've got a girl and even if I didn't, I don't really want the attention," I confess, my voice steady, not wavering in the slightest.

I expect her to take the hint and leave, maybe even apologize for all the over-the-top flirting. I even wonder if she'll be mad and storm off. What I do not expect is for her to double down and put her hands back on me. Her finger is making its way from my shoulder to my hand and my skin crawls, repulsed by her actions. "See, I knew I could make you quiver for me."

My mouth opens so I can rebuke her, but out of the corner of my eye I see Caity looking none too pleased at the situation, and now I'm pissed. I don't want this woman groping me and I don't want her making my girl question my commitment to her. I don't get a chance to tell her any of this, though, because before I know it, Caity is marching up to the table and slapping Tiffani's hand away from me. She turns to face the waitress and rises to her full height, looking mad as hell. "You need to step away from my man. First of all, he's taken. Second, he said as much and asked you politely to not touch him. No means no, and you need to respect that." Caity crowds into Tiffani's personal space, and the petite blonde backs down in the face of such an intimidating force. "Do we have an understanding, or do we need to take this outside?"

Tiffani holds her hands up in surrender. "No, no.

We're good." She turns to leave, but Caity steps in front of her, blocking the way.

"Where do you think you're going? You need to apologize to Noah," my girl insists, her voice strong and unyielding.

Tiffani turns around reluctantly. "Sorry. It won't happen again," she mumbles, looking embarrassed and still a little scared of the redhead next to her.

"You're damn right it won't," Caity states, stepping out of the way and taking her seat next to me with a huff.

I slide my arm around her shoulder and pull her close to me. "Thank you for that. You're my hero," I tell her sincerely, kissing her temple and rubbing her shoulder.

Her frustrated expression clears and she snuggles in closer, grabs my hand, and interlaces our fingers. "You're welcome. Even cowboys need saving now and again."

I chuckle. "That they do, and I like that you were the one to do it. I've never wanted that woman's attentions and now maybe that you've scared the ever-loving crap out of her, she'll take the hint." I rub my thumb across her hand. "Would you really have taken things outside?"

She snorts. "I would have, though I'm not sure how much damage I could have done." She looks up at me. "I probably would have just shoved her, run back inside, and locked her out."

I bark a laugh. "That would have been entertaining at least." I continue to rub her hand and lean in closer to her. "You know, watching you get all riled up like that and defending my honor was hot."

"Really?" She eyes me skeptically.

I run my nose along the shell of her ear. "Oh,

yeah. Really hot," I whisper.

Her free hand moves to clutch my thigh under the table and she squeezes it when I nip her earlobe. "Can we get the food to go?" she asks breathlessly.

"Darlin', that's just about the best idea you've had all day." I grab her hand and we head to the bar to place our to-go order. We stare intensely at each other the entire time we wait for our food and as soon as we have it, we're out of there. However, by the time we get around to eating it, the food has long since gone cold.

Chapter Twenty-Three
Caitlin

The San Francisco air chills my skin as Noah and I walk around the city. We came here straight after school on Friday to spend the weekend in the city before the 49ers game. Our first night was spent having dinner near Fisherman's Wharf before heading to Ghirardelli Square for dessert. It was amazing and we're doing a little more exploring today. We already stopped by the public library and I introduced Noah to a few of my old colleagues. They seemed genuinely happy for me and it was nice to see them, even if we hadn't really kept in touch. Walking around the large library was like stepping into another world, another life. It's still an amazing place, but I find that my little high school library suits me much better, especially since I have made some great friends there and I get to see Noah every day.

The last few months have been amazing. We've spent every night together since that first time he stayed over after Amelia and Gabe's wedding. After a couple of weeks, we just called it what it was and moved him into the house with me. He didn't have much to bring, but we made sure to make the space as much his as it was mine, shopping together for a few new pieces of furniture and some decorations. He's even had Owen and Gabe over for some of their game nights. They let me join in once, but I was banned after beating them all at Mario Kart. That works out just fine for me because I get to hang out with Amelia and Madi, who it turns out is also pregnant. Most of our time together is spent on baby stuff, but I don't mind because I love kids and can picture having some of my own soon. My eyes move over to Noah who is always by my side. As we walk through the city toward our next destination, I can totally imagine him with a little brown-haired, hazel-eyed boy or girl on his shoulders as we have fun as a family.

"Do you want kids?" I ask, unprompted.

Noah stops in his tracks and looks at me. "What brought on that question, Caity-bug?"

I lift a shoulder. "I don't know. I hang out with Amelia and Madi a good amount and that's kind of all we talk about. I just wondered where you landed on the subject." It's probably something we should have discussed before now, but no matter what his answer is, I'm sure we can figure things out.

He lifts our joined hands to his mouth to kiss the back of mine. "Yes, I absolutely want kids." He gets a wistful smile on his face and looks at me. "I can already picture you with a little baby bump, our red-haired little girl clinging to you as you read her a story. I can't wait for that to happen," he tells me.

I smile and blush a little, liking his answer and that he pictures our kids taking after me. "I can't wait for that either," I admit with a grin.

"We could always head back to hotel and get started right now if you like." He winks and I laugh, dragging him toward Golden Gate Park instead.

"As much fun as that sounds, I'm still on birth control and I want to go see all the stuff I never made time to when I lived here." That includes almost every touristy thing we're doing this weekend. There was always just something about the idea of going to all these well-known and crowded places alone that seemed a little sad to me, so I mostly stuck to my routine and a few local haunts.

We continue to walk, taking in the sights and stopping at the odd shop or two, until finally we make it to the edge of the park and head to the Conservatory of Flowers. We step inside and the humidity is a nice relief from the cold outside. I peel off my coat and enjoy the feel of the warm air against my skin. I'm glad I decided to braid my hair today because all the moisture in the air is going to affect it. I look over at Noah and he's lost his coat too, revealing a snug navy henley and dark jeans. I still never really get over how good he looks in just about everything and I take a moment to appreciate the view.

"Look as long as you like, darlin'. I can stand here all day if you want me to," he says, smiling and shifting his body this way and that to show off.

I walk up and kiss his cheek. "I could stare at you all day, but I also want to see some pretty flowers. How about we walk around here and the rest of the park and maybe we can stop by the hotel for an afternoon nap?" I lean in to whisper near his ear. "Then we can both strip out of these clothes and stare all we want."

He looks over at me. His face is flushed and not from the heat of the room. "Let's get this show on the road then, shall we?" He grabs my hand and we proceed through the different rooms, commenting on the various flowers and plants. I take a few pictures on my phone and Noah sneaks one of my behind while I'm bending over to get the name of a particularly gorgeous flower.

"Not cool, Cowboy," I say, frowning at him to hold back my smile. I love that he's so into me. Never in my wildest dreams did I think any guy would be as wildly attracted to me as Noah is, and I am soaking it all in even if I pretend to be annoyed about it.

He lifts a brow. "What? I need something to remember that sweet rump by when you're not around," he says, taking another picture before pocketing his camera.

I laugh. "We work together and live together. I'm

always around." Noah pulls me into his body and wraps his arms around my waist.

I rest my head on his chest and he kisses the top of it. "I know, but even that isn't enough sometimes."

I look up at him and smile. "Awww. You aren't sick of me yet?" I ask, already knowing the answer. There might have been a time in the past that I was worried about him getting tired of me, but it's not something I even think about now.

"Don't you know, Caity-bug? I'll never get sick of you." He leans down and kisses me lightly on the lips. "I love you, darlin'. I want you around me all the damn time."

"I love you too." I squeeze him in a hug. "I guess that means I'll have to learn football so I can be your assistant coach and go on road trips with you."

"Hmmm. I like the idea of you on the road trips with me, but I also like winning games, so I'll pass." I step back and punch him in the arm. He pretends like that actually hurt and rubs it. "Sorry, sweetheart. You are good at a lot of things, but football is not one of them," he says with a sad smile.

"Fair enough. I guess I'll just have to be okay with you sneaking pictures of my butt then," I say with a smirk.

He nods. "Yes, you will. Now, let's check out the rest of this place before I sweat to death. It's like a sauna in here."

I chuckle and we move along to the final room, gazing at the flowers and just generally having a good time. Noah's right, though, it is getting a little too warm in here and I could use the fresh air. "I'm good if you are." He nods and we head back outside.

The cold air is like a slap in the face, but a welcome one. It helps dry my skin which had become a little sticky from the warmth of the conservatory. I shiver and end up putting my coat on after only a minute, but Noah looks like he is enjoying the change of temperature. "This feels so good. I'm burning up inside," he says, fanning his shirt open and closed to get a little breeze going.

I look at his face and it is looking pretty red, so I steer him over to a bench where he sits down with a plop. "Here, let me get you some water." I reach for the backpack he insisted he needed to carry. I know he loaded it up with water and snacks to help keep up our energy as we walked the city.

He snatches the backpack and clutches it to his chest. "Nope, I got it." He unzips it and grabs a water bottle, taking a big swig. "That helps a little. It was hotter than blue blazes in there," he says as he wipes his brow with the back of a hand.

I'm a little concerned because yes, it was warm, but it wasn't ridiculously so. "Are you feeling okay?" I reach up and rest the back of my hand on his forehead. "Maybe you're getting sick."

He shakes his head. "No, no. I'm okay. I just need a minute to cool off and shake the nerves."

Nerves? "What are you nervous about?" I ask. As far as I know, we have nothing going on this weekend except fun and football, so I'm not sure why he's so anxious all of a sudden.

His eyes widen. "Said that out loud, did I?" I nod and he wipes a hand down his face. He looks around. The trees and grass are still green despite it being December, thanks to the coastal location of the park. I try to see what he's seeing and look around. I'm not sure what he's looking for, but by the time I turn back to him, he's staring at me with a small smile on his face. "I wanted to do this while we walked around the Japanese Tea Garden, but I don't think I can wait any longer."

"What are you talking about?" I have no idea what's going on, but I'm not too worried. Everything with Noah always turns out perfectly.

Noah opens the main compartment of the backpack and pulls out a rectangular box wrapped in Christmas paper. "I got you an early present," he says, his voice quivering just the slightest bit.

He hands the package over and it feels hard and solid under my fingers. It doesn't take a genius to figure out that he got the librarian a book. Its cliché, but I don't care because I am that cliché librarian with more books that she can read in one lifetime. "You didn't have to get me anything. This weekend is special enough."

He scratches the stubble on his jaw. "Well, truth is, Caity-bug, I've actually been wanting to give you this for a long time." He nudges my knee with his. "Go on, open it."

I smile and tear at the paper. I turn it around and it's a copy of *The Wedding* by Dorothy West. "Thank you! I haven't read this one." I turn the book over in my hands, it's surprisingly light.

Noah clucks his tongue. "Well, here's the thing, darlin'. I'm afraid you won't be reading that book anytime soon," he tells me.

"Why not?" I open the hardback cover to see that all the pages have been hollowed out and inside the cutting is a small, black velvet box. I stare down at it, knowing exactly what it is, but I also want to hear him say the words. "Is this…?"

Noah grabs the box and goes down on one knee in front of me, opening it to reveal a square-cut emerald set in a yellow-gold band. It's simple yet elegant, and I love it instantly. My eyes well up and I glance over to Noah. "The moment you came back in my life is the moment I stopped going through the motions and started living again. I have never felt more loved, more understood, more myself than when I'm with you. I love you more than I could ever say, but I will try to make it clear every day for the rest of my life if you'll let me. Will you marry me, Caity-bug?"

A tear spills over and I flick it away, laughing as I tackle him to the ground. "Of course I'll marry you, Cowboy." I lean down and kiss him as he clutches my back. I am one hundred percent causing a scene, but if the clapping and whopping I hear is any indication, the small audience we have doesn't really care. I break the kiss and lean back to look into his eyes. "I love you too."

"Yeah, the tackling me into the grass kind of led me to believe that." He cups the back of my head and pulls me down for a longer kiss. After a minute, I realize we're still on the ground in a public park and pull back, shuffling myself onto the bench. Noah stands up and dusts off his jeans before joining me. He grabs my left hand. "May I?"

"Please," I say as I beam up at him. Noah slips the ring onto my finger and I stare down at it, not quite believing we're here, but so incredibly happy we are. Eleven years ago, I was sure I would never feel love again, never want to open myself up to that kind of pain, but I was wrong. I got my second chance at happiness with the person I have loved all along.

Epilogue
Noah

One Year Later

The Graham's house is a little noisier than it has been in years past, the additional sounds coming from the two babies currently being held by their respective daddies. Ten-month-old Mateo Hernandez wiggles in Gabe's arms, no doubt wanting to get down and crawl along the floor now that he's mobile instead of being forced into a high chair. Four-month-old Chloe Graham sleeps peacefully as Owen rocks her back and forth from where he's sitting at the dining room table. It's been interesting to watch my two best friends become fathers. I wondered if it would change them as people, and it has in a way, but for the better. Gabe is more flexible and patient than he was in the past, and Owen is more mature and responsible. It makes me curious as to how I'll change now that I'm married with a baby on the way.

Caity and I got married in a small ceremony over the summer. Our friends and surrogate family gathered in the Shakespeare Garden at Golden Gate Park. Caity thought it would be fun to get married in the same park where we got engaged, but we opted for a much prettier venue instead of the random bench I proposed at. We talked about inviting her parents, brother, and my dad, but in the end we opted to just stick with the people who knew us best. For our honeymoon, Caity and I went to Switzerland. I know she had planned on traveling if she hadn't decided to stay in Sun Valley, so I wanted to give her a small piece of that. We chose Switzerland because it had one of the world's oldest and most beautiful libraries, the Stiftsbibliothek Sankt Gallen, for her, and an American football team called the Zurich Renegades for me, as well as all the cheese and chocolate we could handle. We had a wonderful week there and I look forward to taking more vacations with her. Though, those will have to be a little closer to home now that Caity is six months along. We decided to not find out the sex of the baby, wanting it to be a fun surprise.

I reach over and rub my hand on my wife's growing belly. "How's my little peanut doing?" I ask to both her and her stomach. I love talking to my baby even though I'm sure they can't understand a word I'm saying.

My wife groans and shifts on the chair next to me at the Thanksgiving table. "Your little peanut is not so little and is currently kicking me in the ribs," she complains, rubbing underneath her chest.

I lean down to talk to her belly again. "You be nice to your momma now, little one. When she's uncomfortable, she gets cranky and takes it out on Daddy." Caity slaps my arm, but she's smiling because she knows I'm teasing. That woman is baking our little bun in her oven, so she can get as cranky with me as she wants.

"Here we go," Arthur Graham calls from the head of the table where he delivers the large, golden turkey. The Grahams have always been gracious enough to invite me for their holidays and it's even more fun to come now that I have my own special someone to bring along. Arthur and Sara have been as welcoming to Caity as they have been to me, and we couldn't be happier with the found family we've created.

"Before you start carving that, dear, can I just say something?" Sara asks her husband.

"Go ahead, love. Your little speeches are always better than mine anyway," he says, his eyes glowing with eternal love for his wife.

Sara blushes but waves off the compliment. "I just wanted to say that I am so thankful you could all join us today. I have always loved my family, but that loves grows with each new member. I am so full of love and gratitude that I could just burst. Each of you is such a special part of today and we are so happy to have you here." She sniffles.

"Aw, that was so sweet, Sara," Madi says.

"Yeah, Mom. We love you too," Amelia tells her. Gabe nods his agreement as he tries to calm his son who will not stop wiggling.

"And you didn't even brag about how you finally got to extend the dining table," Owen teases.

"Hush now." Sara slaps at his shoulder. "Now hand me my darling granddaughter so I can snuggle her while you eat." Owen readily hands off his kid to fill his plate and we all chuckle.

We eat and chat, having a wonderful time. We go around the table taking turns saying what we're grateful for and when it's my turn, I don't even have to think twice about it. "I'm grateful for second chances. I got the love of my life and a baby to boot. There's nothing I'm more thankful for than them." Caity leans over and kisses my lips briefly and a chorus of "aw's" break out around us.

Soon enough everyone moves on to other conversation and Caity leans over to whisper in my ear, "I'm thankful for you and our little boy too."

I lean back and look at her with a furrowed brow. "Little boy?" We agreed not to find out the gender, so I'm a little confused.

Her eyes widen and she bites her lip for a moment. "Oops," she breathes out, a worried look on her face.

"We're having a little boy?" I ask, feeling happiness at the thought of my little man in her belly. I would be happy with a boy or girl, but I'm excited to know for sure now. The suspense was killing me a bit.

She nods with a grimace. "I'm so sorry I spoiled it for you. I couldn't stand not knowing and I called the doctor's office last week to find out." She grabs my arm and looks into my eyes. "Are you mad?"

"Mad?" I chuckle and pull her into a big hug. "Darlin', I could never be mad at you, especially not for being excited about our baby." I turn to the table and announce, "We're having a boy!"

Everyone erupts in applause and congratulations and as I look around the room at all the wonderful people, my eyes land on my pregnant wife whose smile lights up the whole room. Yes, I am definitely thankful for second chances.

****

Noah

Five Years Later

Peals of laughter hit my ears as we step out into Gabe and Amelia's backyard. They're hosting our annual Halloween party this year and my family has once again showed up in our superhero costumes. Caity talked me into doing DC this year, so I'm Batman to her Robin. Our oldest, Sean, is The Flash and our two-year-old daughter Bridget is dressed as Supergirl.

Sean looks up at me with big hazel eyes not unlike my own. "Can I go play with Matty?" I ruffle his auburn curls and nod for him to go ahead.

He runs off and Bridget turns her big green eyes

on me, reaching her arms up. "Pick up carry, Daddy?" she asks in her sweet little voice.

"Sure thing, honey." I pick her up and snuggle her close. Her brown pigtails smell like Play-Doh and cheddar crackers, a combination that isn't at all appealing. With a grimace, I glance over at my wife. "I think this one needs a bath later."

Caity gives me a look. "That one needs a bath every hour. I swear I thought our boy would be the one to get into everything, but he's a little rule follower unlike this cutie." She reaches over and gives Bridget a raspberry on her cheek, causing our little girl to giggle wildly.

A loud rumble comes from her diaper and I stiffen. "Uh-oh. I think someone just delivered a package," I say with a frown. It seems like all my kid does is poop.

Caity laughs and takes her off my hands. "Let me. I need to use the bathroom anyway and I can get this little lady cleaned up too." She coos at our daughter and walks inside.

I look over at Gabe who is currently passing off his youngest son to his mom who looks like she's in heaven with a little baby dressed as a pumpkin on her lap. She tickles the chin of their one-year-old son, Antonio, as Gabe joins his wife near the playset. Amelia pushes their three-year-old daughter, Sylvie, who they named after Gabe's late grandmother, on the swing.

"Higher, Mommy," she calls to Amelia, her fairy costume flying around her. It looks very much like the one her mother is wearing.

I spy Sean hanging out with Mateo near the oak tree in the corner. It looks like Mateo is showing Sean all the cool features of his fake sword that go with his knight costume. With my kids occupied, I wander over to Gabe.

"Where's your costume, party pooper?" The man hates to dress up for Halloween and always has the world's easiest costume.

He taps the printed shield on his t-shirt. "Right here. You finally stopped wearing that Captain America costume, so I figured it was fair game," he says with a smile.

"That's hardly the same thing," I tell him. "You could put in a little more effort."

"Look," he tells me, his eyes tired. "I have a one-year-old and am lucky if I get more than two hours' sleep in a row. Forgive me for taking the easy way out."

Amelia looks over at him as she continues to push Sylvie. "I would have found you something," she tells her husband.

He leans over and kisses her temple. "I know you would have, *querida*. But you already have so much on your plate, I didn't want to bother you about a costume."

"Bullshit, you just hate dressing up," I chuckle as I call him out in front of his wife.

Sylvie's eyes light up. "You said a bad word, Unca No."

I get the evil eye from Gabe and hold my hands up in surrender. "I'm sorry, Ms. Sylvie. It was an accident. Can you ever forgive me?"

She giggles. "You funny, Unca No." I take that as a yes and smile at the brown-eyed little girl.

I hear my wife come out of the house, holding Bridget's hand as they walk toward us. My daughter breaks from her momma and runs to me. "Swing, Daddy."

"All right, little lady." I plop her down on the swing next to Sylvie and gently push her as she babbles at the older girl about nothing in particular.

"Where are Madi and Owen?" Caity asks.

Amelia takes out her phone. "Um, they should be here any minute. I got a text twenty minutes ago saying they'd be a little behind since they had, quote, 'a poo emergency'."

"Was it Owen again?" Arthur calls from the porch swing and slaps his knee at his own joke. He and Sara sit and rock back and forth, enjoying the crowded space filled with all their grandkids. The two of them fully retired three years ago and sold off the pub. Gabe, Owen, and I still go every now and then, but it isn't quite the same and we don't enjoy being away from our families much anyway.

As if on cue, Owen opens the side gate and steps through. "Ha ha, Dad." He and his family are all dressed as various characters from *The Princess Bride*, their one-and-a-half-year-old son, Bailey, looking especially cute with a fake mustache to portray Indigo Montoya. It doesn't take long for him to rip it off and start putting it in his mouth, though.

"Nuh-uh," Madi tells him before plucking it from his hands and teeth. She reaches in her pocket and gives him a teething ring instead. "Sara, can you hold this little guy while I run to the ladies' room, please?"

"My pleasure," Sara says with a grandmotherly smile, reaching up to snag the little boy.

"Thank you," Madi says before running into the house like her hair is on fire.

Owen escorts his other two kids, Chloe and Sophia, to the playset. Both girls are dressed as princesses but don't let their dresses prevent them from climbing up and heading down the slide. When Owen stands next to me, CI lean in and keep my voice low. "Madi's pregnant again, huh?"

He looks at me, his eyebrows nearly touching his hairline. "How did you know?"

"Madi running to the bathroom like that means one of two things. She's either super pregnant and has to pee, or she's barely pregnant and has to barf." I slap his back and cluck my tongue. "It doesn't take a genius to figure it out."

He sighs. "Yeah, I don't know how she puts up with it. I hate seeing her so sick all the time," he says with concern for the woman he loves.

"Well, you could just stop knocking up your wife," I offer.

He groans. "I know, but every time she asks for another kid I just can't say no to her. Besides, I think this will be our last one."

"Famous last words," Gabe mutters and Amelia pinches his side. "Ow."

"That's what you get. Besides, we both agreed we wanted three." Amelia rubs the spot she pinched and pushes her daughter some more.

"That was because I had conveniently forgotten what it was like to get up every three hours." He looks at Owen. "You sleeping at all?"

Owen takes a deep breath. "Yes, actually. I'm covered with spit-up or poop half the time, but my kids do manage to let me get a solid seven," he brags.

"I hate you," Gabe and I both tell him.

"What are you complaining about?" Caity looks at me as she grabs Bridget down off the swing. "This one sleeps through the night."

"She doesn't." I kiss the top of my wife's head. "You just sleep like the dead and never hear her wake up."

"Really?" I nod and she smiles at me. "You can wake me up to help out."

"Nah, you need your sleep," I remind her.

Amelia gasps. "You're pregnant again?" Her eyes

are glistening with happiness before the news is already confirmed.

"How did you get that from what he just said?" Caity shouts at her.

"I don't know, I just guessed." Amelia shrugs.

"Cat's out of the bag I guess." I rub my hand on Caity's barely there tummy. "Hunter baby number three is coming sometime next May."

Madi comes out of the house just in time to hear my announcement and claps her hands. "Yeah! I have a baby buddy for this one too," she says delightfully, touching her own stomach.

"Awww, I want..." Amelia starts, but Gabe quickly shakes his head at her. "You're no fun," she tells him, kissing his cheek

"Get me more sleep, then I'll be fun," he assures her.

Sean and Mateo run up to our group. "Can we eat now?" my son asks. "We're starving and we need adequate fuel to energize our bodies for trick or treating."

"Someone's been listening to their dad when he coaches," Caity says.

I chuckle because he is the best little assistant coach I could have asked for. "Sure thing, kiddo. Let's eat."

The rest of the evening is spent with talking, laughing, and have a wonderful time with our friends. Our kids have a blast together and we're all so happy to have created this sense of family, not just for ourselves, but our children as well. I may not have been raised with the family I wanted, but it all worked out because right now I have not only the family I wanted, but the one I needed as well.

The End

SYDNEY SCOTT

EVERNIGHT PUBLISHING ®

www.evernightpublishing.com